# The Amish Amateur Detectives

Terri Downes

Published by Trellis Publishing, 2021.

THE AMISH AMATEUR DETECTIVES

**First edition. July 8, 2021.**

Copyright © 2021 Terri Downes.

ISBN: 979-8224243297

Written by Terri Downes.

# THE AMISH AMATEUR DETECTIVES

## TERRI DOWNES

Jacob had always enjoyed getting to the bakery before it opened. The baker, Aaron King, would start his work well before the dawn, and by the time opening hour rolled around the air would be sweet with the scent of baking bread.

Back in the months preceding Elizabeth's death, Jacob had had to start his day as early as possible, to get all the chores done so he could also work and take care of his wife. He had always tried to time his visit to the bakery so he could be the first one in. Not that Aaron was great company, but it was a small pleasure that often improved the otherwise dreary days.

This morning, however, he was not the only one here.

Jacob almost didn't recognize Rosemary when she rounded the corner on the other side of the bakery. He had hardly seen her since her own spouse had died, a year ago. As she smiled slightly in greeting, Jacob noted that she looked different – although he couldn't quite put his finger on why.

"You're back from your – sister's place?" he asked, trying to make polite conversation in the quiet as Rosemary joined him by the door.

"My brother's," corrected Rosemary. She lifted her face to the early morning sunshine for a moment. "And yes, I got back a week ago. Is Aaron running late this morning, do you think?"

"I guess he must be."

As she stood in the pale gold of the morning light, Jacob could finally see the difference in Rosemary. She had always been so gaunt and pale, her cheekbones standing out and her eyes in hollows. Now, she had gained weight, her skin rosy and clear, her posture strong.

Elizabeth turned and caught Jacob's eye. He quickly turned back to face the door. He had not realized he was looking at her.

He chided himself. Since when had he started looking at any woman like that? He had not given thought to anything of that nature since he married Elizabeth. And after her death, he had determined he never would again. So far, it had been an easy oath to keep.

Elizabeth was pretending she had not seen him looking.

"Why did you decide to come back?" asked Jacob, determined to fill the silence. It was probably the quiet that was leading his thoughts to wander like this. "It's been – what, a year?"

"Just about," said Rosemary. "My brother and sister in law were very good to have me, but I missed home."

"It was nice that you were able to get away for a while," said Jacob.

"It helped clear my head." Rosemary paused delicately. "I guess you weren't able to take any time after Elizabeth passed?"

"No, not really."

"I'm sorry."

Rosemary looked properly at Jacob this time, and they shared a real smile. Jacob felt as warmed by this as he did by the sun that was now reaching the top of the trees.

He looked up, squinting in the light. The sun was, in fact, very high...

"Where is Aaron?" said Rosemary, voicing Jacob's concern. "Do you think something happened?"

"No... I shouldn't think..." Jacob paused. "Why, do you?"

Rosemary flushed slightly, ducking her head.

"Oh, I always think the worst," she said quickly. "I'm sure I'm panicking for no reason."

Jacob frowned at her. "You're panicking?"

"No. I mean, I'm worried. It doesn't matter." Rosemary bit her lip. "I'll just go around the back and knock at the window. He might have lost track of time."

"I can do that," offered Jacob.

"Don't worry," said Rosemary, already heading for the side of the building. "It's just me being silly, I'm sure it's all right."

By now, however, Jacob could see that Rosemary was really quite worried. He, too, was starting to feel concerned. He knew that since Elizabeth's death, he was more prone to jump to the worst possible conclusions. Perhaps Rosemary was doing the same, after her own bereavement.

But even if that was the case, that didn't mean she was wrong. Jacob followed her down the side of the bakery.

Rosemary was knocking at the window, her face pale with worry. She turned and saw Jacob, and tried to force herself to smile.

"He's not there," she said.

"I know," said Jacob. "I realized I couldn't smell anything baking."

"Oh, of course. Perhaps he's ill." Rosemary hesitated. "I'll stop by his house later. I'm friends with his wife Mary, she might need help."

Jacob nodded, looking at Rosemary carefully.

"You're going to go there now, aren't you?" he said.

"Yes," said Rosemary. She lifted her chin, almost as though she was defying someone. "I might be making a fuss over nothing, but I want to be sure."

"That makes sense," said Jacob.

Rosemary blinked at him. "It does?"

"Sure. Aaron's house is on my way home, I'll go with you."

Jacob could not have said why he made the offer. Perhaps it was because he still could not stop looking at the way Rosemary's skin was glowing in the sunshine. Maybe it was because she had smiled at him, sweetly, not out of pity like so many others who tried to be nice to the poor young widower.

Yet as they started to walk, Jacob could not take too much pleasure in the fresh early morning or his pleasant companion. He was starting to feel, for no reason he could describe, as though something were really wrong.

He tried to tell himself that he was just imagining things. This worked, right up until he saw the body.

***

It had been Jacob's idea to call the local sheriff, when they had not gotten any answer to their knocking at Aaron's front door. He had headed back to the woodshed, where Aaron's emergency phone was installed, and made the call.

As she waited for him to return, Rosemary stayed by the front door. She could help but think of how long it had been since she was last here. Mary and she had been close, when they were younger, sharing secrets and diaries and first loves.

Then they had both married those first loves with little thought, and had both suffered the consequences. Rosemary had never spoken about her life with Michael to Mary, but she had seen enough to recognize that Mary had the same problems.

Rosemary placed a hand against the wood of the front door.

She should have written to Mary more often. But after Michael had died, all she had wanted to do was forget.

It was from her vantage point up on the porch that Rosemary saw Jacob leave the woodshed, and start back toward the house. She then saw him stop at the corner of the shed, and double back, as though he had seen something in the yard behind the little wooden building.

She walked toward him, watching as he stopped suddenly and remained completely still.

He turned back toward her when she was a few yards away, and held his hands out.

"Don't," he said. His voice was choked. "Don't come any closer. Stay there."

Rosemary did as he said, but she had already caught sight of the yard beyond him, behind the shed. The figure lying face down on the ground, surrounded by a pool of darkness.

Hours later, Rosemary was still having trouble getting the image out of her mind. She was sure, as she looked across at Jacob on the other side of the police station, that he was also struggling. His face, when he had turned to stop her, had been awful. And then he had had to go over to the body – Aaron's body – and check for life, even though they had both known there was none to be found.

"Excuse me, ma'am." The officer who had taken Rosemary's statement stood at her elbow. "I can take you back home now."

"What about Jacob?" asked Rosemary at once. It felt odd to feel such concern over him, having never had a real conversation with him before this morning.

"Your friend has to have his fingerprints and DNA taken," explained the officer. "Because he touched the body. It'll be a while. Do you want to wait?"

Jacob looked over the sea of desks and met Rosemary's eyes. She remembered, suddenly, the odd warm feeling she had had when he looked at her this morning. She had smiled – *smiled*, of all the ridiculous things, after she had promised herself she would never smile at any man, after Michael.

"No, it's all right," Rosemary said quickly.

She wanted to stay – which meant she needed to leave, and fast. She would talk to Jacob when he returned to town.

As she left the station, she saw the sheriff, and halted. He stopped as well, smiling sympathetically at her.

"I heard you did well, giving your statement," he said, with a nod of approval. "I was sorry you and your friend got caught up in this."

"Has there been any news about Mary? Has anyone seen her?" asked Rosemary.

"I'm afraid not." The sheriff frowned beneath his dark moustache. "But I don't want you to worry. I've been connected with your community for years, and I won't rest until we get to the bottom of this."

He gave Rosemary his card – since when did law enforcement carry cards, she wondered – which read "T. Williams, Sheriff," along with a phone number.

Rosemary thanked him and left. She could, indeed, remember often seeing the sheriff around town, checking in with the local families. He was obviously trying to assure the Amish community that they could rely on the local police – although Rosemary personally preferred the calm, detached professionalism of the officer who was now driving her home, to the sheriff's familiarity.

On reaching her home, Rosemary did not even bother going inside, immediately heading to her aunt's house instead. Her aunt was her nearest family, and exactly what she needed at this moment.

Rosemary had always relied on her family. When things got bad at home, she always had somewhere to go. Her aunt and uncle had supported her throughout all the most difficult times with Michael, and had been the main reason she had wanted to return home after staying with her brother.

It did not take long to explain what had happened to her aunt. By the time Rosemary was done, she was already in tears, as the tension that had snarled in her mind receded and let the waiting emotions through.

"It was just so awful – and so sudden, he was just lying there, he didn't even look like a person – "

Her aunt listened, stroking Rosemary's hand and offering cups of sweet tea.

"I am sorry you saw that," she said, as Rosemary grew quiet. "But I am glad for poor Mary that you thought to go to the house. If you hadn't, no-one would have known she was missing."

Rosemary nodded, wiping at her eyes. Maybe Mary was still alive. Maybe they would find her.

****

Jacob sat up so suddenly he nearly rolled out of bed. He could feel heat along his limbs as sweat sprang up, the nightmare image still vivid in his mind.

He took a few deep breaths and lay back down. He had hoped that the night after he had found Aaron would be the only night he struggled to sleep. But it had been two days, and he was still waking up every few hours.

It didn't help that he kept seeing police cars all over the place, and people kept stopping him to ask about what he had seen. The memory was not allowed to rest – and neither was he.

Jacob kept his eyes open, afraid of what he would see if he closed them.

*Aaron's body, lying there. The rock beside it.* The pictures were ready to spring up at any moment.

After a few minutes, Jacob figured he might as well get up.

He completed his early morning work before the sun had even thought of brushing the sky. He wandered back to the house from his small pasture, then walked right past it and out onto the road. He did not feel like eating, and did not want to lie down and risk falling asleep again.

After a few minutes, he spotted someone walking toward him on the road. When he recognized Rosemary, he wondered whether he might have fallen asleep again.

Rosemary looked just as beautiful this morning as she had done the other day. She was not smiling any more, but she looked at Jacob with an open expression, as though they were friends.

"This must be Providence," she said as she reached him. "I was just thinking that I hadn't seen you since the police station."

"No, no, I guess not," said Jacob.

"I was wondering how you were."

Jacob paused, trying to rub the exhaustion from his eyes. "Me? What do you mean?"

"Have you spoken to anyone about what happened?"

"The sheriff came by yesterday."

"I don't mean like that," said Rosemary. "I meant about what you saw. It can do terrible things to you, to see something like that. It helps to talk to someone."

"I'm fine," said Jacob at once.

Rosemary looked at him, her expression doubtful.

"You look like you're about to fall over," she said.

Jacob sighed. "All right, I've been having trouble sleeping. But I'm sure it won't last. Besides, there's no-one to talk to."

"No-one at all?"

"I don't have any family here, and Elizabeth's folks moved away after she passed."

Rosemary nodded thoughtfully. "Well, you can tell me."

"But you were there. You know what happened."

"I don't know how you're feeling," said Rosemary. "Tell me."

He could not have explained why, but Jacob did as she said. They walked as he talked, trying to describe his thoughts and feelings over the last couple of days. Somehow, he also ended up talking about what it was like to see Elizabeth after she died. Then Rosemary talked about Michael's death.

After an hour or so, they both realized where they were headed. They stopped in the middle of the road.

"We shouldn't go back there," said Jacob.

"You don't have to," said Rosemary, looking ahead at the baker's house. "But I think – I think I need to. I want to look at the ground where we saw him. I want to be able to look at it."

She spoke so firmly that Jacob didn't question her, and he only hesitated for a moment before following her.

They did not reach the house, however. As they got to the front yard, Jacob slowed, trying to work out whether he really wanted to do this or if he was just following Rosemary's lead. She paused and turned back, her expression soft.

"You don't have to do this," she said. "Jacob? Are you all right?"

Jacob was staring off to the side of the house, at the thicket of trees that led to the deeper woods beyond. The greenery was too dense to walk through, and Aaron had always treated it as a fence of sorts.

But now, there was a gap. Jacob went to examine it, hearing Rosemary follow him quietly. He bent down and looked at the broken branches and underbrush that had been trampled. Recently.

"Someone came through here," he said.

"You don't think – you think it might have been whoever killed Aaron?" asked Rosemary breathlessly. "We should call the sheriff again."

"Of course," said Jacob. "Wait. Look." He pointed at a scrap of fabric, caught on a twig.

"That's from a dress," said Rosemary, leaning closer. "It might be Mary. She might have seen what happened and ran away."

"Then we definitely need to call the – wait, Rosemary, what are you doing?"

Rosemary had already started to push through the undergrowth, following the broken trail.

"You can't do that," said Jacob. "They said it was important not to touch anything that might be evidence."

"But if Mary came through here, she might have been hurt," said Rosemary, stopping and looking back at Jacob. "And she would have been here two days already. She might be lying somewhere, waiting for help – we can't delay. Or I can't. You can go back and call."

She turned around and continued pushing through. Jacob looked back at the woodshed, where the phone would be. Then he sighed and started after Rosemary.

"All right, I'm coming. Here, let me go ahead, I'll push the branches back."

"Thank you." Rosemary stepped aside to let him past.

The trail was barely there, made by nothing more than one person moving in a hurry. It was slow going to push through the bent and splintered branches, and Jacob and Rosemary remained quiet for a few minutes.

"Thank you for coming with me," Rosemary said after a while.

"I wanted to help," said Jacob, slightly offended that she might think otherwise.

"Of course," said Rosemary quickly, falling silent again.

Jacob looked back at her, over his shoulder. She was looking down at her feet, as though nervous. It was not the look of fear that should have accompanied a trek towards possible danger. Instead, she looked like she was scared of *him*.

Something deep shifted in Jacob. A memory. Somewhere in the past, he had heard someone talking about Rosemary's husband Michael's unpleasant behaviour. Or a few different people, it might have been, over the years.

He had a temper, some said. A resentful one, always looking for reasons to be offended. Liked to be in control.

Was this was Rosemary had experienced at home?

And was this why she looked so much more healthy and peaceful, now her husband had died?

Maybe she was expecting to be treated the same way as she had been by Michael. Jacob cleared his throat, looking ahead.

"Look," he said. "There's the road. You were right, Mary might have come this way. Good thinking."

Rosemary said nothing, but Jacob caught her surprised look at the compliment. Before he could think of anything else to say, Rosemary stopped and stared at something on the ground.

"What's that?"

Rosemary picked it up. It was a notebook, with most of the pages blank. On the first page, there was an address, a date, and a time.

"This is Aaron's address – and the date and time say two days ago, at nine in the evening," read Rosemary. "That would have been – didn't they say that was when Aaron died? The night before we found him?"

Jacob reached out and turned to the next page, breath catching in his throat.

"What's this address?" he asked.

"I don't know," whispered Rosemary. "Somewhere in the city, it looks like."

The killer might have made these notes for himself, with Aaron's time and place of death. So where was he heading next?

***

Rosemary placed a hand on the wall behind the telephone to steady herself.

"I'm sorry, what did you say?" she said to the officer on the other end of the call.

"I asked you how on earth you got Sheriff Williams' home address," came the snipped, tinny reply. "We don't just give out that information. Who told you?"

"I found it written in a notebook," said Rosemary. "I know it sounds strange – is the sheriff there?"

"No, he didn't come in this morning," replied the officer. "He sent a message that he was sick, but he's been out of contact since then. What's this about a notebook?"

Rosemary explained what she had found, and promised to wait at her home until someone was sent to see her.

Just to check, she dialled the number on the card Sheriff Williams had given her. There was no answer.

She wandered back to her house in a daze, to find Jacob waiting in the kitchen with the coffee she had insisted he drink to keep him awake.

"You think whoever killed Aaron might be after the sheriff as well?" asked Jacob, after she had explained.

"I don't know," said Rosemary, sitting down at the table and reaching blindly for her own cup. "They said he was sick. Or he sent a message saying he was sick."

"What if someone else sent the message?" said Jacob. "What if – " he broke off, imagining possibilities he did not want to speak.

"The killer might have realized the sheriff would be the one to pay the most attention to the case," said Rosemary. "He's always around here. They might have seen him and decided he was a threat."

"That might be the reason," agreed Jacob. "But that doesn't give any explanation as to why Aaron was killed."

Rosemary peered at him from across the table.

"What do you mean? Are you trying to work out why he was killed?"

Jacob flushed slightly. "I'm not trying to do the police's job," he said. "But with the sheriff gone, and Mary still missing, I can't help but wonder whether time might be running out."

Rosemary nodded. "I feel the same. I keep imagining Mary trapped somewhere, or hurt... I wish I'd gone to see her that night. I kept thinking about going over, since I got back, and I didn't."

"Why would you wish that? Then you would have been in danger too." Jacob frowned.

"I don't know that. I might have been able to help. And if I could have helped, but I wasn't there, then it's my fault that Mary – "

Jacob held up his hand, palm out.

"Rosemary, please don't. I can see that you're worried about Mary, and you've been very brave with all of this so far but I can't let you start imagining that you're to blame."

"But – "

"No."

Jacob's tone was gentle, much gentler than Rosemary could ever remember Michael being when he corrected her about something.

Jacob was also looking at her, watching her response, while Michael would have talked to her while looking away.

He was always so ready to be angry with her. Over imagined slights, or mistakes she had made. Any time she answered back. There had not been much violence – nothing that would show. But there had been pushes, and prods. He would stand up close to her, towering over her, reminding her that he could do more if he chose.

Jacob was still looking at Rosemary, his hands clasped over the top of the table.

"Thank you," said Rosemary, unable to think of anything else.

Jacob looked pained. "You don't have to thank me for telling the truth," he said.

Rosemary smiled at him. He smiled back, and she felt that odd warmth again. Before anything else could be said, she heard her telephone trilling out in the shed. She went to answer it – and in a few minutes, the moment she had been sharing with Jacob was forgotten.

"What's wrong?" Jacob asked, as she left the shed. He had followed her out, this time, and waited in the garden while she spoke to the officer.

"They can't send anyone out to get the notebook, or look at the trail we found. There was a big car crash on the highway, and all the officers are busy. We have to wait until tomorrow."

Jacob placed his hands on his hips and blew out a big puff of air.

"I don't know about you," he said, "but I don't want to wait."

"No, me neither. But what can we do?"

The only thing they could think off was to walk around and ask if anyone had seen the sheriff, in the hopes they might find out where he had been heading to last.

"He said he would be going around the community asking questions," Jacob reminded Rosemary, as they knocked on the third of her neighbor's doors. "Someone must have spoken to him."

But that neighbor, like the previous two, had not seen him at all.

"Strange," said Rosemary. "What were they doing for the past few days, if not investigating?"

She tried to think about this, and not about the odd impression she and Jacob would be making on everyone, walking around together and asking prying questions. Hopefully everyone would understand that it was just their concern for Mary – and possibly the sheriff – that was behind their strange behavior.

Everyone went along with their questions, however. Right until they got to the house nearest to Mary and Aaron's.

Jeremiah and Sadie Fisher answered the door together. Rosemary often wondered if the elderly couple were joined at the hip, as they never did anything apart.

They both gave her the same raised eyebrow when she mentioned Mary still being missing.

"It was a terrible shame about Aaron," said Jeremiah, his voice thin and reedy. "And mighty unsettling, them living so close."

"But if the sheriff had come around here, we would have told him not to bother looking for Mary," added Sadie.

"What on earth do you mean?" asked Rosemary.

"We can't spread rumors," said Jeremiah.

"The police will need to know," said Jacob.

"Well, I suppose they oughtn't to keep looking for her if she's not missing," Sadie said, looking at Jeremiah, who sighed and nodded. "We think she's run off with that fellow."

Rosemary stared at them. "What fellow? You don't mean – Mary? She would never – "

"We saw enough to know the truth," said Jeremiah, sniffing. "She was sinning with some fellow, some English fellow. Been going on for weeks now. Months. We never saw his face, but we saw the car going by all the time."

"She already had a foot out the door. If she found Aaron dead she must have figured she was free to go and do whatever she liked," added Sadie.

"But that doesn't mean that's what happened," said Jacob, nearly shouting with frustration. "She might have been hurt as well."

He did not say the awful thought that he must surely have shared with Rosemary – that the affair had been what led to Aaron's death. Maybe Mary's suitor had grown tired of waiting.

Jeremiah and Sadie shrugged in unison. They did not have any more information to give, and Rosemary and Jeremiah left soon afterward.

Rosemary stood on the road outside their house and pressed her hands against her eyes.

"Is it true?" she murmured. "How could I not have known?"

"She would have hidden it from you," said Jacob.

"I was her friend," said Rosemary. "I should have been able to tell something was wrong. If only I hadn't stayed away for so long – "

"Rosemary," said Jacob, his voice faintly chiding again. "Don't do that. It can't be your fault."

Rosemary dropped her hands from her eyes.

"All right," she said. "It's not my fault. But I've had enough of the secrets."

"What are you planning to do?"

***

One of the reasons that Jacob had assumed he would never marry again was that he was sure he would never find anyone else like Elizabeth. She had been the sweetest, softest, gentlest person Jacob had ever met, and none of the women he knew compared.

What he had not anticipated was what might happen if he met someone who was completely, entirely different.

Not that Rosemary was not kind, or sweet. She was – in fact, Jacob could not remember the last time anyone had ever been concerned about his welfare the way she had been, these past few days. But even in that, she was different to his wife.

Elizabeth would never have come right out and asked him to just tell her what he was feeling. She would have waited, perhaps asking leading questions until he told her himself.

Elizabeth probably wouldn't have run into the woods on the trail of a potential killer. She certainly would never have suggested breaking into someone's home, no matter how good the cause. Yet here Jacob was, climbing after Rosemary through Aaron's kitchen window.

"What are we looking for?" he asked, glancing back at the police tape on the door nervously.

"Mary and I always kept diaries, growing up," said Rosemary, already heading out into the hall and up the stairs. "I'm pretty sure she carried on writing in hers."

"You didn't keep yours?" asked Jacob, trailing after her.

"Not much longer after I married. I – " Rosemary hesitated on the threshold of Mary and Aaron's bedroom. She glanced back at Jacob. "I was just writing the same thing every day. There was no point."

Jacob did not ask her what she had been writing. He followed Rosemary into the bedroom and helped search for the diary. After half an hour, it was found behind a loose skirting board under the bed.

Rosemary opened it at once. "There was no point looking if we don't read it," she said, catching Jacob's concerned look.

"I know," said Jacob. "But you should start at the end, not the beginning."

"Oh, of course."

Rosemary paged through the book to get to the most recent months. Her hands started shaking as she read what was written there.

"She was having an affair," she said, a quiver in her voice. "She doesn't mention him by name, but it's clear. She talks about running away with him."

Jacob closed his eyes for a moment. "Does she say – "

"There's nothing in here about hurting Aaron," said Rosemary at once. "She just says she's going to wait for her chance and escape."

"Escape?" said Jacob. "Escape what?"

Rosemary looked at him for a moment, as though the answer should be obvious. Like she knew all about what Mary needed to escape. Then she looked down at the page. Jacob asked no more questions, letting her read. He thought darkly about what he might do to Michael if he was still alive.

"Here," Rosemary said eventually. "She writes about where she's supposed to meet the man, when she runs away. A cabin in the woods..."

"Which woods?" asked Jacob. "Not these ones by the house, surely."

"No, I think on the mountain..." Rosemary frowned. "She mentions that they're used for tourists, that she... hold on." She paged forward. "She says *I can't believe I'm going to stay somewhere I used to sew quilts for.*"

"Quilts?"

"We used to make and sell quilts to those holiday cottages up in the valley," said Rosemary.

"So that's where she is now – or where she was." Jacob thought hard. "She could have gone through the trail in the woods we found, to the road, and met a car there. That road leads up to the valley."

Rosemary snapped the book closed. Her face was set, her eyes hard.

"Then that's where I'm going too."

***

For some reason, Rosemary had not been surprised when Jacob had insisted on accompanying her. He had not even demanded that she explain her determination to find Mary herself. Although he had insisted that they call the police before they called a car to drive them to the cottages.

He was now sitting quietly on the other side of the backseat, watching the scenery that was sliding past too quickly to see.

Rosemary tried to remember if they had ever been friends, back in the old days of youth group and buggy rides. He had never asked her to ride, always having had his sights set on the beautiful Elizabeth. But Rosemary seemed to remember that he had not used to be so sturdy and strong. He had changed. Perhaps through caring for Elizabeth. Or perhaps he was just reacting to the odd situation they were in – though she suspected it was more than that.

Jacob looked over, catching her eye. He smiled, just briefly, and Rosemary did not have to wonder any more why he was here.

Could this really be happening? Could this be what came out of all this darkness?

"Thank you for coming with me," she said quietly.

"Of course," Jacob replied at once.

"You must think it very silly."

"Not at all. You want to be there for Mary," said Jacob. "Even if she has done something terrible, she deserves to have a friend there when the police come."

"Yes," said Rosemary. "I'm surprised you feel any sympathy for her, considering – what she's done."

"We don't know if she had anything to do with Aaron's death," said Jacob, lowering his voice so the driver could not hear.

"Even so," said Rosemary. "She's in sin with whoever this man is she ran away with."

Jacob sat quietly for a moment.

"I can't judge her," he said. "Besides, I have no idea what it is like to be driven to such a thing."

Rosemary looked down at her lap. She wanted to tell him that she knew exactly what it was like, but she did not know how.

"I – " she hesitated.

"I know," said Jacob. "I know. I'm so sorry."

Rosemary's breath caught in her throat. She turned to the window to hide her tears – not from Jacob, but from the driver. She buried her face in her handkerchief until she felt the car rolling to a stop.

She got out quickly, drying her eyes as Jacob paid the driver.

They were on a driveway that led up into an open space, around which was dotted the small cottages. A few of them had cars parked alongside, clearly belonging to vacationing couples and families. There were a few lighted windows in the gradually deepening twilight, but no one to be seen outside.

Rosemary stood and looked around. For every lighted window, there was a car. Those with darkened windows were uninhabited.

Except for the last cottage, the one further up the hillside than the others, sitting by itself next to a copse of trees.

"That one," she said, pointing. "I think she's in that one."

Jacob nodded, and started walking up there at once. Rosemary followed.

She knew it should not be too much to expect, that Jacob should listen to her and respect her opinions. Not all men were like Michael – who would not have listened to her at all.

Who was she fooling? He never would have come with her in the first place, and he would have forbidden her from coming herself.

Jacob would never be like Michael.

Rosemary could not help but smile slightly at Jacob as they stood on the top step of the cottage, waiting for someone to answer after they had knocked.

She felt the smile drop as though it had never been there, however, as soon as she saw the figure behind the rippled glass.

Mary's face was guarded when she opened the door, presumably having seen that the two people on the step were Amish. She held her chin defiantly as she looked down at Rosemary and Jacob.

"I'm not coming back," she said. "You can't make me."

"Mary," said Rosemary gently.

Mary turned on her heel and walked back into the house. She was wearing English clothing, a bright summery dress with a splashy floral print. It looked too big for her. Rosemary wondered if the man she was with had bought it for her.

Rosemary and Jacob followed, leaving the door ajar. Mary stopped in the middle of the small living room, turning to face them with her hands held up in a halting gesture.

"Don't even try it, Rosie," said Mary. "You know – you know what I've been through. I can't go back to it."

Rosemary felt her cheeks pale at Mary's reference. Jacob cleared his throat quietly.

"We didn't come to ask you to return," he said. "We wanted to make sure you were all right."

"Oh, did you? That makes a nice change, someone caring," said Mary bitterly. "Well, I'm fine, so you can go home, and tell Aaron he's never going to see me again."

There was a brief silence.

"What?" demanded Mary, as Jacob and Rosemary glanced at each other.

"When's the last time you saw Aaron?" asked Rosemary.

"The night I left," Mary tilted her head defiantly again.

"The man you're with," said Rosemary. "He was supposed to fetch you? And – and Aaron wasn't supposed to be there."

"But he came back and caught you, didn't he?" added Jacob, catching on to what Rosemary had realized.

"He would have found out sooner or later," said Mary. "I had intended to send him a letter. But yes, he caught us, and I ran off. Tom stayed to defend me, and then he joined me later."

"Did... did *Tom* tell you what happened?" pressed Rosemary. "Did he tell you how he got away from Aaron?"

"He stood his ground," said Mary. "He knows what he's doing."

But now she had started to look doubtful. Her eyes shifted between Jacob and Rosemary, as she tried to understand the meaning behind their questions.

"He knows what he's doing," repeated Jacob slowly.

"Yes," said Mary, wiping her palms on the skirt of her dress as though they were sweaty. "And just so you know, he's on his way back here now, and he won't be happy to see you. So if I were you -"

Jacob suddenly slapped a hand against his head.

"What is it?" asked Rosemary.

"We need to go," he said. "We shouldn't have come. We need to go now."

"Why?"

"Tom," he said, nodding up at Mary. "Thomas Williams."

"The sheriff?"

Jacob nodded. Rosemary felt as though someone had poured iced water into her chest. She also felt very, very stupid.

"Of course," she said, closing her eyes. "Of course it's him."

"That explains why no one has heard from him," said Jacob. "He hasn't been investigating. Why would he?"

"Investigating what?" asked Mary, hands on her hips. "What are you talking about?"

"He didn't tell you how he got away from Aaron, did he?" said Rosemary.

Mary's mouth tightened. "I didn't ask."

"You weren't curious?" asked Rosemary. "And you didn't wonder why you hadn't been followed?"

"We've been hiding out," said Mary. "No contact with anyone."

"And no talking with the neighbors," guessed Rosemary. "Otherwise they might have mentioned what they had heard. The news."

"What news?" asked Mary.

Rosemary looked at her. Mary stared back for a moment, then broke eye contact, looking away.

"You know, don't you?" said Rosemary. "You must know now what he did. Why we're here."

"He hurt Aaron?" asked Mary, her voice small.

"He did more than that," said Jacob.

"I'd do it again."

In the time it took Jacob and Rosemary to recognize the voice, Tom had already come through the door and shut it behind him.

He did not need to make any threatening movements, with the gun clearly visible on his belt. Jacob stepped slightly in front of Rosemary nevertheless – a pointless gesture, but one she still appreciated.

Tom ignored Jacob, however, focusing instead on Rosemary.

"Mary told me about you," he said. "She told me you were friends. She told me how jealous she was of you, when your husband upped and died just like that, leaving you in peace."

Rosemary swallowed against the sudden dryness in her throat.

"I didn't have anything to do with that, it was a heart attack," she said.

"Do you know how many times I prayed for something like that to happen?" asked Mary. "I needed it just as badly as you."

"I – I never told you –"

"You didn't have to," said Mary. "I didn't have to tell you either, did I? About my life at home? But you knew anyway. I could tell."

"You could have come to me, Mary," said Rosemary, hot tears threatening to fall. "I could have helped."

"How? You left, for a whole year," Mary almost shouted. "You weren't there. Tom was."

"And I'll always be there," said Tom, looking over at Mary from his position blocking the door. "I was going to tell you about Aaron, sweetheart. I didn't want to upset you – it was an accident."

Mary nodded, still glancing nervously between Rosemary and Jacob.

"I'd have thought you of all people would understand," said Tom, mirroring Mary's resentful look towards Rosemary.

Rosemary felt her breath curdling in her lungs. She did not know what to say. And Tom was still standing by the door, hand hovering near his weapon. She opened her mouth, but nothing came out.

"Of course she understands."

Rosemary looked in confusion at Jacob as he spoke, but he did not look back at her.

"Why do you think it's just us here, and not the police?" he asked.

Tom's expression flickered uncertainly.

"Rosemary just wanted to make sure Mary was all right. But neither of us would ever blame you for what happened, even if you had gone there with the intention of ending it." Jacob drew himself up a little. "I certainly understand. You're right about Rosemary's husband. He deserved a slower death than the one he got."

Rosemary's heart thudded painfully at this awful remark. She knew – she was *sure* – that Jacob could not mean what he was saying. But Tom was nodding along.

"So you two are what, together now?" Tom asked.

"Yes," Jacob replied without hesitation. "I'm just sorry it didn't happen sooner, when I could have helped her."

Now Rosemary knew he was lying. When Michael was still alive, Jacob was still married to Elizabeth. But if Jacob was lying, it was for a reason.

She stepped out from behind Jacob, seeing his shoulders tense as she did so.

"I know I was lucky, with Michael dying so suddenly. I was – I was going to leave him." She twisted her hands together. "I had a plan. I was going to go and stay with my brother. My aunt was helping me."

Mary looked sceptical.

"And I know it's my fault you didn't have anyone to talk to, Mary. I'm sorry, I am. I'm so glad you've managed to – to get away from everything."

Mary stared at Rosemary. Rosemary held out her hands, trying not to look desperate. Mary hesitated for a moment, then moved forward, clasping them tightly. Rosemary drew her into a hug. She was unable to disguise the shaking of her shoulders, but hoped Mary wouldn't notice.

"I just wanted to know you were all right," Rosemary said.

Jacob glanced out of the window.

"I think the car might be back for us soon," he said, moving for the door.

Tom stepped in his path. Jacob halted, but kept his expression calm.

"It's all right," he said. "We won't leave until we've straightened everything out. But we'll need to tell the car to go without us."

Tom looked over at Rosemary and Mary, still hugging. Rosemary tried to look as though she wasn't paying attention.

"I'll tell the driver," said Tom.

"Sure," said Jacob. "No problem. We'll stay here."

As Tom walked out of the cabin, Rosemary broke away from Mary.

Mary looked at Jacob and nodded approvingly at Rosemary, then headed for the bathroom.

"Ugh, I'm all blotchy," she said, a trembling voice belying her attempt at light-heartedness. "I'll just be a minute."

As soon as she was out of sight, Jacob beckoned for Rosemary to follow him, and slipped into the adjoining bedroom. Inside, he gestured for her to stand with him against the wall furthest away from the front of the building.

"What –"

Jacob shook his head. Rosemary fell silent.

Outside, she could hear something. The sound of a car, pulling into the long driveway between the cottages. No, it was the sound of more than one car. They were driving fast, then stopping suddenly. The police had arrived.

Then there were the sounds of shouts, and of someone running.

The bathroom door opened.

"Rosemary? Where are you? What's –"

There was a shot. Rosemary heard Mary gasp and run to the door, flinging it open. Her cry reached them easily.

"Tom!"

Rosemary covered her mouth.

"You think he's –"

There were more shouts. Tom's voice could be heard, calling down curses on the officers who had apparently caught up to him as he ran.

"He's not dead," said Jacob, the relief in his voice evident.

Mary was outside, calling out to the officers to let Tom go. Rosemary shivered.

"You were trying to get him away from us?" she asked.

"I thought he might try something – take us hostage, or try to shoot his way out – when the police arrived," said Jacob. "And I knew they wouldn't be too far behind us."

Someone called out from the front door.

"Police! Anyone in here?"

"We're back here," Rosemary called back.

Someone entered, holding a gun ahead of them. It was the officer Rosemary had spoken to at the station.

"What on earth?" said the officer, looking Rosemary and Jacob up and down. "What are you two doing here?"

"We were trying to find Mary," said Rosemary.

"You found a good deal more than that," said the officer. "You could have been shot."

"Was that the sheriff, shooting just now?" asked Jacob.

"As soon as he realized we'd work out why he was here. He didn't even hesitate," said the officer, shaking his head. "Like he thought he was in a Bonny and Clyde movie. It's insane."

Having made Jacob and Rosemary promise not to leave their spot in the bedroom until called for, the officer went back outside.

"What made you think he would turn violent?" asked Rosemary, leaning back against the wall and looking at Jacob. "If he only killed Aaron by accident?"

"He didn't," said Jacob. "I saw the body. There was a rock."

"From the wall by the shed, I know," said Rosemary.

"There were footprints in the dust," said Jacob. "They tracked from the spot where Aaron was lying, to the wall and back again. Aaron must have been knocked down, and Tom went to get the rock..."

Rosemary cringed away from the images forming in her head. She remembered Jacob's haunted expression when he talked of what he had seen.

"You didn't tell me about the footprints," she said.

"I was trying to leave out as much as possible," said Jacob. He sighed ruefully. "Not that it seems to do much good, trying to protect you from anything. We still ended up facing down a murderer all on our own."

"But I would have been alone, really alone, without you, here" said Rosemary.

Jacob smiled at her, then pulled a face, looking away.

"I'm sorry for what I said, in there, to Tom. I wanted him to trust us enough to leave us alone. He needed to think we were on his side."

"I know," said Rosemary. "You didn't mean it."

"I tried not to," muttered Jacob. "About Michael, I mean."

Rosemary looked down.

"I'm sorry," Jacob said at once.

"I understand, said Rosemary. "I also wasn't sure of how much I meant what I said. I had wished, so often, to be free of Michael, that when it happened, it was almost like I had caused it."

"But you didn't." Jacob sighed. "It's hard to find a place to stand on this. Whatever she did, Mary should never have been in this position to begin with."

"Someone should have been there to help her," said Rosemary.

"Someone should have been there to help *you*. Both of you."

Rosemary nodded. "I – I was telling the truth about leaving."

She was careful not to look at Jacob as she spoke.

"I know," said Jacob.

"And?"

"And what?" said Jacob. "Like I said, I can't judge anyone. And even if I could, that's not something anyone could pass judgement on. All I can do is be glad that you're safe now."

Rosemary pressed her lips together, feeling tears welling up again.

"There was something I said too – something I wanted to be true," said Jacob.

*You're together?* Tom had asked. *Yes*, Jacob had said.

"I know," said Rosemary.

"And?" said Jacob, his voice hesitant.

"And what?" repeated Rosemary, unable to stop herself from smiling. Jacob smiled back at her from within the gloom, light through the shadows. "I'd say the way ahead is pretty clear."

# ELLEN THE MAIL ORDER BRIDE

SHIRLEY DAVID

## <u>Chapter 1</u>

### *1885, Manhattan, New York*

Ellen was grumpy, because it was the first month into winter and with all the snow outside, she could see no reason why her mother insisted on hauling her to these elite society balls. The Manhattan Society get together was overrated, and she had enough, but never the less she was here, and as they took her coat she looked around. Ellen looked around the ballroom. To the curious onlooker she might seem to be looking at the people in the room with heightened curiosity, and they wouldn't think much of it. They wouldn't because she was on the verge of reaching spinsterhood and still single, clearly. The Manhattan Society had already all but cast her out. She like the freedom that no longer came with their expectations.

It wasn't that she was ugly or even that she had a nasty personality. Not at all!

Ellen had suitors falling all over her. The minute she walked into any room she was the centre of attention. Her looks awed those who laid eyes on her, her grace and elegance made women wish they were her and she was smarter than most men who like to dress up and pretend they knew what they were doing. Ellen was a catch by any standard. Men poor and rich fawned over her, but she thought they were all idiots and when they weren't, she could not be seen with them. It was an infuriating fact. One her mother always said was just her reality.

"Looking for the one?" Her mother, Anna, whispered in her ear as if on cue.

"No mother. I am looking for several escape routes out of here should any number of the men in here who think they are the one attempt to talk to me."

She could hear her mother's exasperated sigh and knew what was coming, so she quickly walked away and lost herself in the crowd. Taking a glass from the waiter who passed her, she walked through the

French doors to the back and out to the garden. The snow fall had eased and the air was crisp and refreshing. It made her miss the one man she had actually fallen for. He had been their gardener, with excellent taste in flowers and eyes that sparkles with adventure and pulled her in. When her mother had found out why she was smiling that much all the time, Anna had not been pleased. The next day she woke up to see the love of her life leaving. He had stayed in town for weeks after looking for work, but her mother had made sure no one else would hire him. A month later he left. She never saw him again, and then two years later his sister sent her a small box with two letters. The box held the broach she was wearing tonight. He had been planning to give it to her as her birthday present, before he was forced to leave. The first letter was one proclaiming his love, and the other was one from his sister explaining he had died from pneumonia in one of the harsh Wyoming winter. She had cried and refused to leave her room for almost a week. She had read stories of heartbreak so profound that it crippled you. Then she experienced it. It changed her, and no man had ever resonated with her like he had. Hence why she was in the snowy garden reading the papers in the lamp light, and sipping a glass of wine, instead of inside smiling to entertain men she wanted nothing to do with.

As the cold got too much to bear without a coat, she when back to the party, but made sure to stay in one of the plant room that was warm enough so she wouldn't freeze. That was where she was as she read an ad in the Newspaper for a wife in Wyoming. The thought appealed to her not just because of a husband. Lord knows being a mail order bride was not on her list of things to do, but it could be a great adventure. At the very least, if it didn't work out she could come back home to her miserable mother.

She didn't bother going back inside where all the other elites were expected to be. She took her heels off, walked on the thin layer of snow that covered the lush grass and hopped across the hedge, ripping her dress in the process. She did not care. She just wanted to get out of there and luckily her carriage was close enough. She gently squeezed the leg of the sleeping driver and he woke with a startle.

"Your mother?" He asked her as he pulled away in the carriage.

"She will be just fine."

Ellen smiled wickedly and chuckled at the thought of her angry mother in the morning. She didn't care. She knew she would be fine.

The following morning she had him take her into town early, and in secrecy she sent a telegram in response to the ad for a wife. The following day an invitation to meet came and in less than a week and with no explanation to her mother, she headed out on the train.

"When will you be back?" Her mother asked her with tears in her eyes.

Ellen loved her mother despite the fact that they couldn't get along and she gave her a long hug and the truth. "I don't know Mom. I just need to get out of here for a while. I will send you a telegram twice per week. If you don't hear from me, send the Calvary."

Her mother laughed. "They won't mess with you. They will regret it."

Her mother hugged her long and hard. Ellen let her. She didn't know when she would see her again, but if all went well, her mother might just be happy she found a husband. For now, she kept the reason for her travel a secret, and looked out the window at New York fading in the background.

### Chapter 2

"Don't forget us," Burt said to her as she walked away. He had become more than her coach driver. In fact, he had held her secrets of her first romance when she had fallen in love. She would miss him.

The whistle blew for the boarding call and she kissed his cheeks. "See you soon," she told him, speaking all kinds of possibilities into being. He nodded and helped aboard the coach. When it pulled away minutes later she waved to him until she couldn't see him anymore, and then it dawned on her. It was clear to her that he was the only family she had left and now she was leaving him behind. She hoped the man she was going to would be a kind and gentle man enough to become her family too. Marriage didn't always constitute that, and she was after all a mail order bride, with a return stamp should he desire that she return to wherever she was coming from.

"Your son?" an elderly woman who had a Bible open, asked from the seat across from her.

Ellen smiled. "No, just a humble little man I had the opportunity of meeting," she said referring to Burt.

"Ahh, these days it is so hard to find men of that sort," the woman lamented. "I only hope he grows in that way."

Ellen hoped so too and said as much.

"I am Freida," the old woman offered her a shaky hand encircled by a rosary. "Please to meet your acquaintance."

"I am Ellen and the same here," she smiled back.

"Heading off to a new life further west?" the woman asked eyeing her suitcase at her foot. She nodded. "Plenty of adventure to be had then."

"Oh good God I hope not!" Ellen exclaimed. "I am hoping for a quiet life, uneventful save for the everyday nuances of survival. Too much adventure will surely cause me death."

The older woman laughed at her proclamation. "Is it that you have had too much adventure already or are you just not interested in any?" the woman asked.

"I have had my fair share of struggles, and I am afraid that adventures of the kind you are talking about kind will bring more to my doorsteps."

"Life is perspective, little one," the old woman began speaking to her with a voice that bid her listen to the wisdom she was about to impart. "And without a little adventure we would all turn to rocks sitting in the same spot staring at the sun each day. Never let it said your youth is wasted on you."

Ellen knew her words to be true, but as the train whistled on its way, she really was hoping it would whistle her away to quiet and easy.

"I don't mind adventure Freida," she began solemnly. "What I fear is that when the joy and spoils of adventure has passed I will be left right where I started and I cannot have that. I cannot be forced to start all over again."

The woman reached a hand across to her and took it in her old palms, calloused with signs of working for too many years. "You should have no fear of anything life throws your way. I have a feeling you are a survivor, and with God by your side be it famine or festivities you will be just fine."

She smiled not so confident in the woman's words.

"Where is your husband?" Frieda asked.

"Never met one. I am hoping the man I will meet at the end of this day's journey will be him."

"Ahh you are a mail order lady," Frieda said her eyes opening in joy. "So too was I once."

"Really?" Ellen's attention perked up as she waited for the woman to impart some sage advice.

"I have one piece of help to give you," Freida began the smile leaving her face. "Make him understand that you are not there to wait on him and serve as a soft place to be bedded every night. You state your purpose beyond that, so he will see you as a valuable addition, and once he has, you will find should anything happen to him you are well taken care of."

Ellen was a bit confused uncertain of what she really was speaking of, but she had a feeling she would only understand through living the reality. They spoke for the hours until she fell asleep, and hours more the following morning for the time that it took them to get to Iowa, which was her first stop, and as the train drew to a halt Freida offered a prayer on her behalf. Ellen was a woman of faith and so she bowed her head in prayer too for the life that awaited her. She could only hope it would be one she would like.

"Be careful," Frieda called after her. "The winters that side are horrible."

She waved with gratitude, but the following day when she made her way to the train station to finish her journey, she was not prepared for what fate would throw her way.

## Chapter 3

### Train station, Iowa

Rex ignored the men shouting at him to stop him as he ran towards the train that was about the pull away. His first thought was that it was too early in the morning to get shot, yet here he was with a bullet in his side and three men after him. He thought he had lost them along with all his money in Wyoming. He thought he had gotten rid of them, yet here they were in Iowa. He had to shake them.

The wound in his side would make that difficult. He looked ahead at the graceful woman about to board the train and shoved pass her and stepped on. The train began a slow chug and as the doors closed behind the woman who was staring at him furiously, he saw the guard stop the men; one brandishing a gun and the other glaring at him through the window.

"Unhand me!" The woman shouted at him.

He realized then that he had gripped her hand. He wasn't sure if it was out of pain or relief, but as the train picked up speed and the adrenaline of the chase wore off, he realized the pain was real. She was gorgeous though, and he could barely take his eyes off her.

He let go out of fear more because he was afraid she would smack him, and then walked away looking for an empty seat. He would worry about the fact that he had no ticket, at the end of the trip when the steward would walk around asking for one. He took a seat in the luxurious leather chair beside the window, and was happy that people were busy settling in. Too busy to notice him, except her.

"No you are in my seat!" The same angry voice sounded and he looked up and into the greyest eyes he had ever seen. She was truly breathtaking.

"That one isn't taken," he pointed across from him. "And I would love your company."

The last two words came out as a coral as the bullet wound in his side reminded him of his presence.

"How rude!" She exclaimed. "I paid for both these seats to avoid insolent people like you."

She was even gorgeous when she was fussing. And for the next few minutes he enjoyed her annoyance, the sound of her voice was soothing, though he didn't hear a single word she said. She dropped a book on the table.

"Get up now, before I call the guard."

He didn't want that at all. He tried to stand but the wound in his side wouldn't let him, and as he fell forward she caught him.

"What is wrong with y-"

She stopped talking as the hand that clutched her for support was covered in blood.

"You need a doctor!" She cried out.

"No!" He said. "If I get off this train they will kill me. I just need to get to Wyoming."

"By the looks of that," she pointed at his side. "You will die long before that."

"Only the good die young," he assured her as he sat back down. This time she sat across from him, but he could see she was scared.

"You will bleed out..." her words trailed off as the guard came by.

"I won't. I have survived worse."

He could see she wanted to say more, but she was trying to decide whether to help him or turn him in. In a few minutes he got his answer.

"Come with me."

It was an order he found himself not wanting to refuse. She took her small bag with her and then they made their way to the bathroom. It was a small space but well adorned with the luxuries of the wealthy. Not at all the bathrooms he was used to in the poorer side of the train. And though he could think of a million inappropriate things to say, he found he didn't want to. He just wanted to listen to her as she cleaned his wound and chided him for begging like a girl when he winced in pain. He was too awed by her and the fact that she pulled a small bottle of vodka from her purse and used that to clean his wound.

"The bullet is still in there. It will have to come out."

He didn't say anything to her. He knew better than anybody else that if it stayed in for the fourteen hour train ride, he would be in trouble. He bit down on her bag strap and tried not to black out from the pain as he shoved his finger into the hole and pulled the bullet out. She just stared at him in shock. Minutes later she finished bandaging him up and told him not to move. She came back with a new shirt and though he wanted to ask her where she got it from, she thought she better not.

When they sat down again, he almost instantly fell asleep.

Hours later she woke him to eat, change his bandage and then gave him some pain killers. She repeated that three more times for the time, then when she woke him the last time he felt like he was on fire.

"Can I get you any help?" She asked as they came off the train and the cold Wyoming winter air kisses his face.

He reeled off an address and just before he collapsed he saw her worried face looking at him. When he woke hours later a familiar face was staring at him.

"Ether?" He asked.

"Didn't I tell you not to get in trouble?"

He smiled and went right back to sleep. He was safe...for now.

**<u>Chapter 4</u>**

*Crestfalls, Wyoming*

Ellen couldn't just drop him off at the inn and leave him. For days she kept going back to find out if he was okay. She didn't even know why, because he was inappropriate and rude most of the time, but she knew that a part of her enjoyed the conversations they had.

He was easy to be around, and his devilish green eyes enchanted her in ways she could not understand. She had all but forgotten the real reason why she was in Wyoming. On the third day she was there, she woke up telling herself that she was off to meet this new husband at hers, but by the end of the day she had sent a telegram explaining she had been held back by the weather. Then she had walked the few minutes from the hostel she had found for herself nestled on the edge of the forest, to where Rex was. Her excuse was she just wanted to check on him and Ether, the old lady she had come to like so much, but she knew better than that.

It was the sound of his voice, and the way that even when he was being rude he was still being kind and gentle. He was a paradox without question, and she enjoyed his company beyond words.

"This is you?!" he asked incredulously the following day as he help up a magazine.

She stalked over to him and grabbed it from his hand. It was a picture showing her on the steps of her inherited mansion shortly after her father died, with an article talking about the empire she would now have to run until her heir came of age. She had marvelled at the article. It was invasive and not all true, now here he was looking at her bemused.

"What are you running from?" he asked. But when he realized she was not smiling at his usual wicked jokes, she saw realization flash across his face. "It's okay. You don't have to tell me, but maybe a Wyoming winter was a bit extreme a time to get away."

She laughed. "Well I was not running away from anything." She knew that was not entirely true, but it would make her feel better for now.

"Will you tell me what you are doing here? It can't be any more embarrassing than why I got shot."

The way he asked, was soothing. It instantly told her that somehow he meant no ill by it. And so she did, watching his eyes get huge as he listened to her story. When he was done, he simply could not believe that a catch like her was allowed to leave New York unwedded.

"Are you secretly a psychopath?" he asked in bewilderment. "That is the only explanation."

She chuckled. "No, I guess I just haven't found the one yet...I think."

He looked at her and walked across to her, tucking a stray strand of her behind her ear. He seemed like he was about to say something, but decided not to. The electricity flowing between them said enough. She pulled away and gave him some excuse as to why she had to leave before the snow started again, and even as Ether invited her, yet again, to their ranch she smiled and gave no response. Being around Rex was stirring up all kind of emotions in her that he had no idea how to handle. And for the next week she stayed away from him, but feeling like an idiot, the following Friday she dawned her coat when the snow eased, and decided to way to the inn. She would use the time to compose herself.

But as she got to the edge of the road, her boots slid on the frozen surface, and the last thing she thought of as her head slammed into the ground, was that she was going to freeze to death without seeing him one last time.

### Chapter 4

"What are you so happy about this today?" Mason asked him as he walked into the wood shop. The cold air blasting outside made him shiver a bit, but he was grateful that the infection form the wound had now healed and he could help out on the ranch again. He was even more grateful to finally be out of that drab inn where Ether worked most days.

"I don't know what you are talking about?" Rex replied, putting the finishing touches on the piece of work he was doing.

Mason circled him, eyeing him suspiciously. "Yes, you have that glow. That deep happy glow you have not had in ages. And considering how foul a mood you were in yesterday, explain yourself."

Rex laughed. "I was just thinking about Ellen. You know? The woman I showed you in the magazine-"

"Wait," Mason interrupted. "You mean Ellen Margo? The Ellen Margo?"

Rex frowned at him. "Why do you say it like that? Nothing is wrong with her!"

He found himself getting upset at the mere fact that Mason could be implying anything in a negative sense about her. He felt the need to protect her and put everybody straight, and it surprised him.

"No!" Mason laughed. "I think she is awesome. In fact many a men would love to get with Ellen Margo. We know she is a catch, and her father was a well respected man in New York. I didn't think you would be so strung up on her though. Nobody thought you were over Emma."

"What?!" Rex was shocked.

"Yeah," Mason said shedding his jacket and taking a piece of wood up to help Rex get ready for his next job. "We thought you would get a dog and call it a day. Is Ellen still in town?"

Rex didn't know what to say to that, because he honestly had not thought any such thing. "Yes, she is. She is staying by the foster hostel at the edge of the woods."

"Is she seeing anyone?" Mason asked

"I don't think so," he replied realizing that he hope she had not made good on her mail order promise. She had run off that day, and he was giving her time, not that the weather was giving him much of an option.

"Is that a bit of hope I hear in your voice, Rex Miller?" Mason teased.

He smiled but kept his eye on his work despite the fact that he could not deny that he was actually hoping she was single. He assumed it since she spoke of the stress she was having with her mother, and had she been with anyone, maybe she would not have been on the side of the river by herself last night.

"I don't know if I am even ready to start dating anyone again," he replied. And that was the truth. Rosemary and Kiera and then Emma's death had made it very difficult for him to look forward to that. Society women were a pain, except Emma. He didn't have to be told Ellen was different though. That was something he already knew.

Their attention was drawn away from that conversation when customers walked in and shortly after Ether, Mason's Aunt and only living relative, showed up with thermoses of hot tea and a whole cake.

"You should take a bit to Ellen," Mason said.

He looked at the snow picking up outside and remembered that he needed to deliver a small cabinet to Bishop George anyway, and he lived a few houses up from where Ellen was staying. He agreed and in less than thirty minutes he was in his way.

He kept practicing out loud what he was going to say to her when he finally saw her again, but he felt like maybe he should really say anything. He was contemplating maybe just not going there when he saw a black lump looking so out of place, pushed next to the fence. As he drew closer he realized it was somebody lying there on the snow covered ground and he quickly pulled over.

His heart fell to the soles amid his feet when he bent over the person and saw it was Ellen.

"Ellen!" He called to her in panic but no response came. Her skin felt cold and it seemed she had been out there for a while. He lightly lifted her into his arms and it took seconds for him to decide that his house was closer than hers, and when he wrapped her in his coat and the blanket on the inside of the buggy, he spurred the horse into a fallow and returned home. Skidding to a halt in the driveway he shouted for help and Ether and Mason came running out.

"I found her on the side of the road," Rex said worriedly. "It's Ellen, and it looks like she might have slipped and fallen. She is really cold."

The next few minutes raced by as they all worked on trying to save her. Then he left her with Ether as she stripped her down and washed her with warm water she had been boiling for soup for dinner. Rex paced outside the door, and when Ether opened it to tell him to get some of Emma's old and warm clothes, he raced down the hall to the room his dead wife's things were. He was back in less than a minute and when Ether finally allowed them in the room, he raced to her side.

"Will she be okay?" Rex asked.

Ether smiled at him. "Seems she did hit her head pretty hard, but she will be fine. We just need to keep her warm. In the meantime I think you need to call her parents. The blizzard has started and there is no way she will be making it back to her hotel today."

It was not until then that Rex realized the storm raging outside. Winter was officially here.

"I think this is fate," Mason said to him.

With that he left Rex to his musing and Rex looked down at the woman he was sure he had feelings for. He didn't care that he only knew her a couple weeks. His whole came alive when she was around. Alive in a way he knew was not just in passing.

"Oh Ellen?" He said drawing his chair closer to her bed and taking her hand in his. "You have to take better care of yourself."

He looked at the sleeping woman and hoped she could hear him, but even then he knew he would be around to look out for her if she couldn't do it well enough for herself. But for now he stayed by her bedside and that is where he fell asleep an hour later.

### Chapter 3
*The fire was creeping closer and the heat was making her sweat through the thin fabric of her frock.*

*Trapped again!*

*That was the only thought Ellen had as she tried to hold her breath long enough to not inhale the smoke bellowing around her. The flames crept closer, and even though she was cold and feeling like she was freezing from the inside out, the flames still managed to burn her.*

*She screamed....*

"Ellen," she heard a gently hand shaking her awake. "Wake up!"

She grabbed at Rex's shirt monetarily disoriented unsure of where she was, but his big warm hands cupping her face and his concerned eyes were enough to tell her she was okay, as a child wailed close to her.

"Just a dream," she said almost like she was convincing herself. "Just a dream."

He nodded his head and behind him she could see the night's sky. "Yes, just a dream."

"Where am I?!" she sat upright in the bed, and that was the worst thing to do. Her unsettled stomach and the pain in her head ensured that all she could manage to do was shove her head over the side of the bed and empty the contents of her empty feeling stomach, into the pan Rex instinctively lifted to her head.

"You have to take it easy," he urged rubbing her back. "You took quite a hit to the head."

"Hit to the head?" she asked confused and disoriented. "What are you talking about?"

"You had a little accident Ellen," he began softly as she rubbed her temples. "Two days ago I found you unconscious and nearly frozen to death on the side of the road. I don't know what happened exactly, but seemed you fell and hit your head. You were almost frozen to death."

It came back vaguely to her and she remembered wanting to walk around and underestimating the winter moods. She should have listened to Frieda.

"How long have I been sleeping?" she asked him instantly worriedly as the baby wailed again.

"Two days Ellen," he said worriedly, while he told her he called her parents but the storm outside didn't seem like it was about to stop anytime soon. "You are okay though. Just rest."

"Thank you," she said, as the child cried again. "You have a child?"

He laughed. "No I wish. That is Mason's son, Christopher. He left him here for a couple days, while he and his wife travelled to see her sick mother. Ether and I are taking care of him."

She smiled. "So I finally made it to the ranch. Just not the way I wanted to."

He chuckled. "You are here and that is all that matters."

She could see that the words came out of his mouth before he had time to stop them, and embarrassment flashed across his face. But for her, hearing those words felt just right somehow. He excused himself and went to get Christopher, who looked at her like she was not supposed to be there, before a smile spread across his face. Ether came in and fussed over her for a bit. When she managed to drink half a bowl of soup and her headache subsided a bit, she reached for Christopher and he willing crawled into her arms. She didn't want to, but somehow she felt safe with Rex right there and she was a bit too tired to fight it.

"Thanks for saving me," she whispered as Chris rested his head against her chest.

"And I always will once you need saving. I have committed to that task for the rest of my life," he joked, knowing that for him it was somehow true.

She laughed and they spoke about the ranch, and how he wished she had seen it before the snow. He told her about the wood workshop and she loved the way his eyes lit up at that. What really spoke to her was that despite the fact that he was wealthy by any standards, he seemed to take most joy from the simply art of carpentry. She felt herself falling in love with him a little as he spoke. And then and there she understood what she had been feeling since she ran into him that day.

This wasn't lust or any such thing. It felt like a coming together that was meant to be. She just couldn't explain it.

He took the child from her arms and walked around her room rocking him to sleep. And Ellen admired just how right he looked. He would make someone a great father someday. As he saw her eyes dropping closed he started to excuse himself.

"Will you stay for a moment?" she asked him acting out of character and patting the space beside her. "Just for a bit."

He nodded and sat in the bed beside her, maintain a respectful distance. She pulled him over by the shirt to the centre of the bed and he laid on his pillow with his arms beneath his face staring at her. She looked back at him with droopy eyelids.

"What was that dream about?" he asked her softly, running a thumb over her cheek bones.

She looked at him and smiled. "A fire. It is always a fire."

She closed her eyes felt his long fingers run through her hair and massage her scalp. She was expecting him to comment but he did not, and now she wasn't sure what to think, but it felt wonderful to feel him there. Maybe this was where she was meant to be. Maybe she wouldn't go meet this man she was supposed to meet after all.

It was virtually unheard of to have a man she was not married to in her bed, but she felt she could be weak for even a moment. She had earned the right to be after everything she had been through. She turned away from him and curled her legs into her chest, knowing the nightmare she had just had was some concoction of what she had been feeling and the dread she feared would again take over her life.

"Thank you," she whispered. She could feel the strength of him shuffle closer to her.

"For what?" he asked. His breath caressing the back of her neck.

"Thank you for being here, for having me here."

His hand rubbed her shoulder in response and she pulled his arm around her. He moved closer to her and rubbed her back protectively, while Christopher slept on his chest. At least for one night she had someone with her. She fell asleep while she prayed and dreamed of a kind of paradise many would find strange.

"Ellen," he said, "you know you will be okay right?"

She thought about it for a moment, but she wasn't so sure. "How do you know that?" she asked.

"Sometimes we all need people in our corner," he said to her. "People are better than no people and I don't know what you have been through but I am in your corner now."

She fought the tears that threaten at his kind words. "But you don't even really know me."

He fell silent, and she had a feeling he knew exactly what she meant. "I don't have to really know you to care. I see you as a beautiful soul who came into my life for a reason and as long as you allow me to, I will be here."

"Thank you," she whispered trying to hold the tears that threatened to fall at bay. "Thank you for being here today and for caring enough to want to help."

For the first time in a very long time she did not feel alone.

"You mean to tell me you have finally accepted that I am here to help?" he asked his breath stirring strands of her hair as he laughed.

She chuckled in his arms feeling the strength of him hold all her broken pieces together. She was really warming up to him, and appreciated the fact that he simply held her without the need to make a move.

"Yes," she whispered back.

When morning broke, hours later, she was alone in bed, but the smell of breakfast was a welcoming scent. Rex was nowhere to be found and as she jumped from her bed in panic she heard his squeals outside. Walking to her window she looked down to see him playing with Christopher on the patio. The snow had eased, and a little fresh air would be excellent for the little boy too. Her heart felt at home, but her mind kept reminding her that she was just a visitor to this little paradise and soon she would have to return to reality.

It was not a thought she enjoyed having right now, and she pushed it away as she turned from the window.

### **Chapter 4**

For the next three days they could go nowhere. Every single time that the snow eased and she greeted the possibility of leaving with a bitter sweet response, it would start right back up again. As the day rolled on Ellen could not help stealing knowing glances at Rex. Whenever their eyes met he would smile or wink and the red would creep from the tops of her toes to her cheeks. She found she needed fresh air more often than she normally would throughout the day. Well what she really wanted to do was click her heels and do the chicken dance, but that would be out of character for her, so she settled with the glow that radiated from inside out.

Mason had not come back from his trip and so they all spent a lot of time taking turns looking after him. Ether managed to teach her how to bake a pineapple short cake, and she had many scintillating conversations with Rex.

"I like having you here," he whispered behind her as she put Chris down for his midday nap.

For a second she thought it might have been the blizzard howling outside that spoke, but when she turned and saw his smiling face staring at her, she knew she had heard him right.

"I enjoy being here too," she replied, and it was the most honest she had been with herself in the last few days. In fact, she had spent quite a bit of time trying to convince herself that she wasn't feeling all the things she thought she was feeling. She had gone to the length and breadth of it all in these little conversations she had with herself, but as she stood looking at him, she knew for a fact that those conversations had been pointless.

She had fallen for this man.

And in a way, she had a feeling she had known all along.

"I don't know how I will ever go back to what my life was after you leave," he said as she stepped out of Chris's room and into the hallway.

"Oh, stop saying that, because you don't mean it," she said looking away from him. He was so gorgeous and strong. He could have any woman he wanted, why would he be taken with her?

He reached for her hand and stopped her midstride, and then he turned her around to face him and looked her directly in the eyes.

"There is a part of me that loves you Ellen," he said stepping up to her. "But it took Mason to point it out and for that I am sorry."

"I don't understand," she said looking at him confused.

He lifted a hand to run soft finger across the scars on her neck and then he smiled. Pulling her towards the stairs where they sat, he started talking.

"He pointed out how different I am when I so much as mention your name."

"Oh so you talk about me?" she smiled mischievously at him.

"Pay attention," he said pinching her nose with a laugh. "You said you came here for a change and a chance of something more, and I have a past that won't let me get on with my life. Maybe, just maybe we were meant to meet each other the way we did."

She smiled, because she couldn't disagree with that logic. She felt like she was exactly where she was suppose to be and for the first time in ages, she felt like maybe, just maybe, all was right in her worlds.

Conversation over the next few weeks detailed his life for her. She was happy he was freely telling her about himself. Most me these days behaved like their existence was to be a mystery. She much preferred the open flow of conversation, and when he told her of the money he lost trying to start a business of his own, and how he tried to gamble to win it back, she didn't here the stories of a man she should not be with. She heard the story of a man who wanted a better future.

"But I will work on the ranch and see if I can pay those debts and then start again," he said smiling at her.

Despite the sincerity in his voice, the collectors came banging on his door two days later in the midst of a blizzard, and when Mason opened the door thinking it was some wayfarer needing help, the gun barrel that point at his head was followed by three strong men who forced their way into the house. After threatening to shoot everybody in the house unless they got their money, Ellen decided to step in.

She ran off up the stairs ignoring the threats they shouted at her, and came back with her purse. Inside it were several notes more than they were owed. The men's eyes glossed over, and when they had stripped her of her jewellery and warned them not to tell anyone, she was just happy when they left the house.

An embarrassed Rex could not look at her as he apologized and promised to pay her back.

"Stop," she whispered to him as she touched his cheek. She looked at him and knew in that moment she would be lost to him forever.

"I am sorry," he said again. But the silence that passed through the room in that moment, told them that he would have a lifetime to make it up to her.

Even as their lips met for the first time, they both knew that through adversity, they had found exactly what they were looking for...love.

# LOVE UNLIKELY

## LOVINA SWANSON

## Chapter 1

Haylee lay in the darkness of her room staring out of the window at the moon that hung low in the sky, her only consort in her lonely life of misery and depravity. Four years after meeting Jase her heart was broken into a million pieces and scattered across the vast expanse of her own insignificant universe. Move on, they said, he's not worth it, they said, you deserve better. What did they know? None of her so called friends could ever imagine how she felt deep down and how utterly destroyed she was when she walked in on Jase in the arms of her best friend, Lucile. Of course the first thing both of them shouted when caught in the act was – it's not what you think! – The most default response.

After Jase pleaded with her and Lucile convinced her that it was an irresponsible judgement error on her part and that it would never happen again, she gave it another shot. She should have known better. Naïve little Haylee, who only tries to see the good in people ended up as the biggest fool of them all and when it happened a second time, she could no longer be ignorant. It was obvious that between the chemical combination of Lucile's raging pheromones and Jase's ego boosted testosterone, she never stood a chance. She had to finally admit to herself that she was never going to find true love, and friendships are feeble pastimes for pre-schoolers.

It's been almost two months since her relationship with Jase ended, and it wasn't long after that, that she also handed in her resignation as an article clerk. Breaking up with Jase and seeing him once in a blue moon she could handle well, but working with him and sharing the same open office day in and day out was a little too much to handle. It amazed her how men in particular, could be so callous and move on without a worry in the world. She had managed thus far, but the more she sat at home she started to feel cooped up like a bird in a too small cage.

She sighed and tugged her blanket over her shoulders and tucked it under her chin as she turned unto her other side, this time staring at her graduation photo. She stood tall and proud, alone in her toga with her rolled up certificate in her hand, no immediate family to share her successes with her. Her mother, or rather adoptive mother had passed away six months short of her graduation that year. Haylee sniffed and blinked away the tears. She didn't cry then and she won't cry now. Finally giving up on sleeping she tossed the blanket back and sat up in bed. Her mom always told her, that every person has left something behind in their past, that sits there and waits until they go back to find it and resolve it. And until recently she had never thought she wanted to go back there. She was only four when she was adopted, a lonely grey mouse stuck in foster care. From the first day she arrived at her new family, she was accepted and spoiled rotten. She never needed for anything in her life, and she never felt as if she was any different to any of the other kids, so why she suddenly felt like digging out the past was a mystery to her, but every day it became more and more pressing. And here at two in the morning, she was stuck between forcing herself to sleep or logging into her email to see if the adoption agency managed to track down her biological mother or family. Insomnia won the battle and she finally made herself a cup of coffee and sat down at her desk and logged into her emails.

Dear Miss Jones

We have managed to track down your biological mother, but it is with regret that we inform you that she passed away a few years ago due to illness. We have however managed to track down her parents, your grandparents. We do however wish that you consider the fact that they may not...

Hayley stared at the email, reading it over and over again, somehow grief evaded her, and it was like reading the sad story of a stranger. What she did learn from this was that her mother was born Amish, and that her grandparents lived in an Amish community in Ethridge,

Tennessee. But even if she knew who they were, what good would that do now? It wasn't as if she could reunite with her long lost mother anymore. But what she might be able to figure out is what type of woman her mother was and what type of life she lived. Maybe it will even shed some light on why her mother gave her up for adoption. As she spent her time reading up on the Amish and their culture, it became more and more evident that her mother may not have had a choice, but this was pure speculation. And unless she took the time to find these things out for herself, she would always be guessing about the woman who brought her into this world.

Besides, it wasn't as if she had anything better to do with her time. She had no job, no love life and no coffee, she thought as she looked at the empty canister in front of her.

That was it; she was going to take the last of her savings and head to Ethridge and find the Lapp's.

Chapter 2

The whole way to Ethridge, Hayley kept wondering if she was making a mistake. She was about to embark on a journey she was in the least bit prepared for. Before she left everything behind, she made effort to reinvent her wardrobe with a few modest outfits just so that she wouldn't look too outrageous amongst the Amish. But even now as she sat in the back of the cab, her heart was beating a million miles a second and she was on the verge of having a nervous breakdown. She had just left behind the only life she knew, not that there was much left of her for her to salvage, but she was somewhat comfortable where she was.

The cab pulled into the small town of Ethridge and stopped in front of what appeared to be a touring business.

"This is as far as I can go missy," the cab driver said and pointed to this meter.

Hayley nodded and fished for cash to pay the cab driver and the moment her bags were offloaded and she stood like a singled out deer in hunting season outside on the sidewalk she wanted to burst out in tears. Whatever was she thinking coming out here?

"Hello, may I help you?"

Startled Hayley nearly lost her balance as she spun to look at the stranger behind her, "Oh-I-um, well, I'm looking for someone," she said and dug in her purse, "Mr and Mrs Lapp?"

"Oh Fredrick and Mary Lapp, yah, they live here. I can take you," the young man said.

"You know them?" Hayley asked in disbelief.

"Yah, well it's a small community we all know each other," he said tucking his thumbs under his suspenders.

Hayley couldn't help but stare, wondering if all Amish men were this good looking. This guy couldn't be much older than her twenty five. And although he was dressed modestly in what she had to assume Amish clothes, he looked reasonably attractive. She was never one for men with hairy faces, but for some reason his beard which was slightly trimmed suited him perfectly. He had ebony black hair with willow green eyes set deeply in his skull.

"If you're done staring..." he said interrupting her thoughts with his brows drawn together.

Embarrassingly she shook her head, "I'm so sorry, I just... it has been a really long day and I've travelled a long way."

"No matter, my name is Duncan," he said and nodded his head courteously, extending his hand.

"Hayley," she said and gave his hand an overly firm shake.

"Well I best be getting you to the Lapp's, the weather is turning foul."

Without notice he started loading her luggage into a carriage that stood nearby and then patted the back of the carriage, indicating her seat.

Who was she to ask questions, she hadn't the foggiest about their customs and every website she visited to learn about them were know-it-all windbags who have made up assumptions. So instead of opposing she hopped into the back of the carriage and sat down.

"So do you know the Lapps?" Duncan called over his shoulder as they made their way into the town.

"I...sort of, actually, I knew their daughter," she lied, she had no clue what their daughter was like. Just because Hannah Lapp gave birth to her, didn't exactly mean she knew her.

"I think you might have them mistaken for someone different, they only have a son, but Kendrick moved to Lancaster with his wife."

Well this was a good start, she thought as she tucked her lip under her teeth, "Perhaps I am confused, but I suppose there is no harm in meeting them. Maybe they might know Hannah Lapp as extended family."

"Hannah Lapp," Duncan repeated, "The name sounds familiar."

The carriage came to a halt and Hayley fell forward along with her luggage and just then the heavens opened up.

"Come!" Duncan called and reached for a sheet to cover her luggage before effortlessly lifting her off the wagon and placing her on her feet, "The Lapp's live here, if you hurry I can wait and take you back to Richland Inn."

"Wait, what do you mean back to town, I need to be here in Ethridge," she protested as Duncan lead her up to the house where the Lapps lived.

"Well if the Lapps won't let you stay in their home, you have nowhere else to stay, unless you want to sleep in the barn."

"The barn?" she asked appalled.

"Duncan, vas in der velt?" an elderly man interrupted as he opened his door.

Duncan immediately removed his hat and clutched it in front of him then looked at her before turning his attention back to the older man.

"Mister Lapp, this is Hayley. She's come to Ethridge to look for..."

Before Duncan could continue Hayley stepped up and extended her hand, "Grandfather?"

The older man's complexion paled, and he exchanged looks with Duncan then looked at Hayley, "You're mistaken," he mumbled and moved to close the door, but then an elderly woman appeared and the expression on her face was one of pure shock.

"Hannah... you look just like her," she said in a trembling voice as her eyes shot full of tears.

"Grandmother?" Haylee said as she stood with her hands folded in front of her.

"Come dear child, you're going to get soaking wet out in the rain," she said as she dragged Hayley into the house, despite her Grandfather's disapproval.

And as she disappeared into the kitchen she heard her grandfather mumble for Duncan to bring her luggage inside.

Her grandparents, she couldn't believe it. She was actually in the very house her biological mother grew up in. Her grandmother seemed far more accepting of her than her grandfather did, but she refused to make any assumptions until she had all the facts. For now she will take the time she had to get to know them.

Chapter 3

A week since her arrival and all she could determine was that her mother, Hanna Lapp went on a Rumspringa and never returned.

"Did she never write to you?" Hayley asked her grandmother one morning after her grandfather left to go to work.

"She wrote to us, but only ever to let us know she was fine," her grandmother said softly as she continued with her sewing.

"But weren't you in the least bit worried?"

Mary put down her sewing and reached out for Hayley's hand, "Yah, we were worried, especially your grandfather, but our laws are different to those on the outside. Hannah made her choice and she had a chance to return."

Hayley sat quietly for a moment and squeezed her grandmother's hand. The short while she had been here in the Amish community of Ethridge, she had found a sense of peace and tranquillity she never felt before. With the exception of a minority of locals who walked wide circles around her, the younger people like her were friendly and very accommodating. She couldn't understand why her mother would have left for good, and trade this life for what lay outside in the world. But then, being on holiday in a strange place was far different that living the life in full.

A knock on the door drew her attention and her grandmother quickly set her sewing aside and went to open the door, and a few seconds later she returned with Duncan in tow.

"Hayley, Duncan is here to see you," her grandmother said smiling.

Duncan was another person she was growing fond of at an alarming rate, but thankfully the walls she erected around herself kept her level headed. She knew that the only reason she felt closer to him than any of the others was because he was the first person she met when she arrived.

"Hi Duncan, what a nice surprise," she said standing up.

"Good day to you Hayley," he nodded tucking his thumbs in his suspenders, "I was wondering if you would like to go to the market today, I have a few errands to run."

Hayley felt the slight flutter of butterflies in her stomach and tugged her hand into her midriff. It would be rather nice to get out a little and get to know other parts of the community, she thought and then nodded.

"It would be lovely, let me get my coat and purse," she said and hurried to her room.

She forced herself not to eavesdrop on her grandmother' and Duncan's conversation and quickly got what she needed before joining them.

In no time they were on the carriage and on their way to the market, this time Hayley got to sit in the front and not like some baggage on the back.

"So how are you enjoying your stay here in Ethridge?" Duncan asked curiously.

"It's nice. I mean, it's very different to city life, but so far I'm enjoying the peace and quiet," she said and glanced out over the landscape.

"Yah, it's very quiet. So did you manage to find out about Hannah?"

"A little," she said, but decided not to elaborate. She didn't want to put the Lapps in any sort of disrepute, but she found it hard to believe that Duncan had no clue about her, but then again, he was probably still a baby when Hannah left the Amish community.

"So will you be moving on then?" he said clearing his throat.

Hayley turned to look at him and smiled, "Not sure, maybe. Tell me about this Rumspringa thing."

Duncan laughed and looked at her, "Well, Rumspringa means to run around, when the youngsters turn sixteen they can choose to go out and experience things outside of our community. It's each one's choice, some do it and some don't."

"Did you ever, I mean did you do it when you turned sixteen?" she asked curiously.

"Nay, I never did. I have all I need right here."

"So you never wonder what lies out in the cities."

Duncan drew the carriage to a halt and then turned to look at Hayley, studying her with those intense willow green eyes.

"Most young men leave because they are not satisfied with their life here, mostly because they are tempted by the modern world, and women," he said and for some reason his cheeks grew rosy.

Hayley tried to hide her smile and coughed softly, "So you never wanted to go find some hanky-panky?"

"Hanky -panky?" Duncan asked and blinked, "What is that?"

"Uh... well meeting women, dating and so on."

Duncan threw his head back and laughed, "Oh no, I had no interest in those things. Not then anyway," he said and then tugged on the reins sending the horse back unto the road, "I always believed that at the right time God will send the right woman my way. I'm a patient man Hayley Jones."

When he looked at her then, she felt her heart flutter in her chest and she immediately looked the other way. Her mind was clearly playing tricks on her; there was no way that Duncan would even consider looking at her twice. She was an outsider for one, and secondly she wasn't exactly a virgin either. And although she still knew very little about their laws and traditions, she was sure the Amish probably had the highest moral values in the world second to nuns.

The rest of their trip was in silence, and a few miles further they finally reached the Amish Country Mall. Hayley was quite surprised by the variety of goods that were sold at this place, but more so how many non-Amish visited the place. It was like a tourist distraction for curious people. And as she stood next to Duncan and the Carriage in her own authentic Amish dress, a sense of pride washed over her. Surprised that she actually felt Amish in some farfetched way, she smiled at Duncan and then headed into the shop. She found it quite amusing that it was called a Mall when all it really had were old antique trinkets and a limited menu of food. There were some items for sale but it was hardly considered anything close to a shopping Mall. She did her bit to get a few items for herself and when she next exited, she found Duncan standing next to her grandfather, both in deep conversation. Instead of barging in on them she took a walk around the store to give them their own time. Her grandfather had hardly spoken a word to her since her arrival and he was still a great big mystery to her. On occasion when she did ask her gran about him, she simply avoided the topic. She wasn't any closer to find out exactly why her mother never came back.

Chapter 4

Duncan couldn't help but admire Hayley, and although she was an outsider, she seemed to adapt quite well to the Amish life. It's been two weeks since he met her, and the more time he spent with her the more he started to like her. The first day he saw her was the first time he ever really looked at a woman. She was modestly dressed in a floral print dress that flowed elegantly down her body to her calves, but what intrigued him most was her shyness. The fact that he had the impulsive need to run his fingers through her long brown tresses was abnormal for him and he quickly stifled that need, by reminding himself that she was an outsider, which helped.

Normally when outsiders visited the Amish communities they stuck to their modern clothes, where the women wore as little as possible. No wonder so many of the Amish boys opted to go on their expedition to the cities, being tempted by the promises that the modern world presented. Two of his own best friends went out to experience the world and all it had to offer, but he never felt that desire or pull to know what happens out there. He was more than content to live this life of simplicity, working on the farm and making goat's cheese. There were many times when he attended the sings and where he contemplated the option of taking a wife, but none of the girls here in Ethridge ever made him feel the way he did now. And he was adamant that if he was going to take a wife, it would be someone who would completely consume his thoughts. He wanted the same love with a wife than his mother and father shared. He had never seen them argue, and they always showed their affection towards each other. And if they could have such a devoted marriage, why could he not have the same?

Duncan was caught in his own thoughts when the smell of burning wood and grass wafted through the air.

"Duncan!" It was Hayley who rode towards him on one of the Lapp's horses, her eyes wide, "Come quick, my grandfather's barn is on fire!" she cried.

In an instant Duncan had called his father and his neighbours, and everyone else he could alert and they were on their way by carriage to the Lapp's farmlands. Up ahead he could see the plume of fire explode into the grey sky. Flames rolled outwards and embers were flying up into the sky.

When he pulled up next to Hayley where she dismounted the horse, he took the reins and handed it to another young man, "Take the horse to my father's barn and keep it there," he instructed and then turned to Hayley, "What happened?"

"I have no idea, we were all having dinner when we heard the loud crash of lightning, and not long after that the smoke was everywhere," she said ringing her hands together.

Duncan's concern for Hayley had to be set aside, and although he wanted to comfort her, he had to attend to the bigger problem.

"Okay, go to the house and stay inside," he ordered as he scooped a bucket of water from the trough.

"But I can help," she protested and reached for a small barrel.

"You've done enough, now go and sit with your grandmother, I'm sure she could use the company."

Her mouth opened in protest but then shut, and with a slight nod, she ran across the field towards the house.

They fought all night to get the fire under control, thankfully the Lord had blessed them with rain to help put the fire out, but all that was left were the charred remains of the barn in the smoky morning air that reeked of burnt wood and straw. His father had warned Fredrick about the tall dead tree that stood so close to the barn. But misfortune led to lighting striking the dead tree and causing it to fall on to the barn. Luckily it was only the barn that burned down, somehow the horses were freed before the barn was completely on fire, and he has the slightest suspicion that it was Hayley's quick thinking that saved the animals. As for the equipment, it was all replaceable.

"Thank you son, if you didn't arrive when you did I would have lost all my horses," Mr Lapp said as he came to stand next to Duncan.

"Nay, that was not my doing. Hayley saved the horses," he said and looked at the older man.

"Hayley saved them?" he asked disbelievingly.

"Yah, she came to fetch me on horseback, I've never seen a woman ride so well, but she came to call me straight away. By the time I got here the horses were already in the fields and Kent took them to my barn."

Fredrick stood quietly for a while rubbing his beard, and Duncan knew that he had his own demons to face. He too had never heard of Hannah Lapp, but spending time with Hayley he had learned a great deal.

"She's seeking your approval," Duncan said crossing his arms as both of them looked at what remained of the barn, "She deserves a fair chance."

"You're right," Fredrick said and then headed towards the house.

Duncan looked as the older man walked away, his shoulders hunched as if he carried a heavy burden, but he knew Hayley deserved a fair chance, she had nothing to do with her mother's disobedience or her choice to give her up for adoption.

Later that day, Duncan stood in his father's barn, grooming the Lapps' horses. The least he could do was make sure that none of them were injured. But more than anything he needed to keep busy so that he could chase the thoughts of Hayley from his mind. Every waking hour was seemingly consumed by thoughts of her, and after her courageous act it was even worse. Now he knew exactly how King Solomon must have felt, being tempted by a beautiful woman.

"Duncan?" he heard Hayley's voice from outside the barn.

"In here!" he answered and tossed the brush in the sack hanging on the wall.

"Oh there you are," she said smiling and held out a basket for him, "Grandma and I baked these to thank you for helping us out with the horses."

Duncan smiled and took the basket filled with cookies, "Thanks, but I think you deserve all the credit, if it wasn't for you these horses would be charred with the barn."

He noticed Hayley blush as she averted her eyes, "I love horses, I had to do something."

Duncan stepped closer and reached out to tuck his finger under her chin, "And you did an amazing job of saving them," he said but his voice betrayed him.

This close to her, he could smell the fresh scent of lavender and vanilla, and although it was just the crook of his finger brushing her unblemished skin under her chin, it was the silk soft smoothness that tempted him more than anything. And without a second thought he stepped in and pressed his lips against hers. Hers were soft, like cotton pillows and although the kiss was brief, it was a defying moment for him. He knew there and then that Hayley was the woman he'd been waiting for all these years.

He broke the chaste kiss but didn't step away from her; instead he kept his eyes locked on hers. It was that moment between two people where words were irrelevant syllables and consonants were fleeting sounds that would never be able to express the emotions that sparked between them.

It was Hayley that stepped away first, and how shyly tucked a strand of hair behind her ear.

"My grandfather said that they will be doing a barn rising this coming weekend, will you come?" she asked softly.

"I wouldn't miss it for the world," Duncan said.

And as Hayley walked back out of the Barn she looked back over at him again and smiled.

Duncan felt like a teenager for the first time, and now more than ever was he determined to make Hayley Jones his wife.

Chapter 5

The barn raising was well on its way, the men from the community had spent most of the morning working and Hayley was amazed by how quickly the barn started taking shape. She heard many stories about this experience and how the Amish are able to build an entire barn in one day, but she had never seen it with her own eyes. Duncan was at the front line of everything. He did the planning and the design, his skill as a builder came in handy and it appeared that young to old admired him, but not nearly as much as she did.

When she first decided to come to Ethridge, finding love was the last thing she anticipated. After her failed engagement to Jase, she had sworn off on ever dating again, but here she was, utterly captivated by Duncan. He was the complete opposite to Jase. He was kind, considerate, a true gentleman and there was something about him that she craved.

"He's a fine young man," her gran said as she handed her the basket of fresh fruit.

Hayley tore her eyes away from the barn and smiled at her gran, "Yes, he is," she admitted.

"You know, Hannah never told us about you until after she gave you up for adoption," her grandmother started, "When she told us your grandfather begged her to withdraw the adoption and rather send you to us."

Hayley sat down opposite her gran at the wooden table, "So you did know about me?"

"Oh yes we did, but your mother had already handed you to your new parents, and we had no way of finding you. That day you arrived here in Ethridge, you were a splitting image of my Hannah."

Hayley's eyes shot full of tears and she reached out to take her grandmother's hand, "My adopted parents were good people, they really looked after me as if I was their own."

"I know, but I can't help wonder just how things would have been if Hannah had come back home," the older woman admitted and lowered her eyes.

"I'm here now though, and you've made me feel at home."

"Yah, yah, I know. I've been trying my best. Your grandfather blames himself for what happened, but he's a good man."

Hayley smiled and then looked back at the men toiling in the sun. Her grandfather was a proud but humble man, and she knew that deep down he cared for her.

By six o'clock that evening, the barn stood tall in all its glory. Brand spanking new as if no disaster had struck it just a week ago, and everyone in the community had gathered to celebrate the event. It was a festive atmosphere to say the least, and for the first time in her life Hayley felt as if she belonged. Over the weeks she spent here in Ethridge learning to bake and quilt, she hardly thought of her life in the city. And the hustle and bustle of peak hour traffic and busy shopping malls was nothing but a distant memory of a temporary life she once knew.

She made a few friends and even the older people had started to like her. Maybe it was due to the fact that she did not come here to dispute their faith or their ways, but she embraced it like any Amish citizen would.

From across the group of people she caught Duncan looking at her, but instead of looking away, she smiled at him, and even when one of his friends tapped him on his shoulder he still looked her way, refusing to drop his glance. She noticed immediately that he no longer had a beard, but that he had shaven, and the sight of him made her knees weak. It was she who first looked away when her grandfather came to sit beside her.

"My dear," he started sounding uncomfortable, "I owe you an apology for my behaviour."

Hayley turned to her grandfather and smiled, "No need, you had a lot to cope with, with my untimely arrival. I should have taken better care to notify you before I just dropped in."

"No, it's not that. I-I never gave your mother a chance to rectify things and for that I am forever guilty, I should have gone to find her."

Fredrick pinched the bridge of his nose and shut his eyes and Hayley knew he was fighting back the tears, she gently placed her hand on his, "The choices we make are our own, and we are all responsible for them, no one can take responsibility for the mistakes of others."

There was a moment of silence, and when her grandfather looked up at her again he smiled tenderly, "You will make a wonderful Amish woman," he said and patted her hand, "And Duncan would choose well to ask for your hand."

"Hayley, come!" One of the girls called and tugged her up by her hand, "You must join in on the sing."

Before Hayley could process the words of her grandfather she was caught smack bang in the middle with a bunch of the younger people, and although there were no instruments, the clapping of hands and the harmonies of voices made the songs come to life. Among the crowd was Duncan, subtly making his way closer to her and the closer he came the more her heart beat out of control and the butterflies that hijacked her insides fluttered up a storm. She might very well be an outsider but she could not deny the fact that somehow providence had claimed a victory.

"Would you spare me a few minutes of your time?" Duncan whispered as he reached her.

"Of course," she said and followed him outside.

Duncan had his hands tucked in his pockets as he stood outside. The moonlight spilled down from the heavens like a silver curtain, bathing their surroundings in silver dust and casting its subtle glow over them. And as Hayley came to stand next to him, they both glanced up into the sky.

"Hayley..."

"Duncan..."

They started at the same time and then burst out laughing.

"You first," Hayley insisted and Duncan smiled and turned towards her.

"Okay, well, I'm sure this will come as no surprise to you, but I thought it best I clear the air," he started clutching his hand in his hands, "I think or rather, I know that I have grown very fond of you, and I know that it may be a little more complicated than usual, but I have spoken to your grandfather."

Hayley stood playing with the string of her prayer cap, coiling it around her index finger nervously. It felt is if her heart was going to jump out of her throat as Duncan went on, explaining how he had asked her grandfather if he would allow him to court her. A few weeks ago, she would never have considered this, but now where she stood under the moonlit sky, with her hand in Duncan's she knew exactly what she wanted.

"And did my grandfather approve?" she asked curiously biting her lip.

"He did indeed, which is why I have gathered to courage to ask you in person," he admitted and smiled.

Hayley shifted her weight and sucked in a breath, she had no idea how Amish dating customs worked. Of all the things she had yet to learn, dating hardly featured and she recalled only briefly spot reading over that section.

"So are we going to be bundling?" she asked innocently and blushed.

Duncan raised his brows and chuckled, "My dear Hayley, you have so much to learn still, no one does that anymore," he said and stepped closer to her and reached to remove her prayer cap.

"Is that allowed?" She whispered softly as Duncan's lips hovered over hers and he pulled the pin that secured her hair in a bun lose.

"What happens between us, and the Lord, is all that matters," he said and then wrapped her lose braid around his hand and kissed her fully on the lips.

## Chapter 6

Hayley stood in front of the mirror, while her grandmother fussed with her long hair. It's been a year since she joined the community and although her and Duncan's feelings for each other were no secret to the rest of the community, they both kept their word to follow the rules and customs as required by the Amish Council.

"So the food is almost ready. Once your Grandfather and I are off to the church service, you and Duncan can sit down and celebrate your betrothal."

Hayley looked in the reflection of the mirror at her grandmother, the woman she had grown to love and smiled, "Do you think I will make him happy, Grossmammi?" she asked.

"Natuurlijk! You're his future and the woman he had been waiting for all this time," her gran reassured her.

After her grandparents left to go to church, where the minister would be announcing the brides to be, she waited patiently at the house for Duncan to arrive. She kept looking at the clock on the wall, it was a unique hand crafted clock made especially for her by Duncan, as a courtship gift. Time however seemed like it had deliberately slowed down, and when she heard the carriage finally pull up in front of the house, she had to force herself to stay calm and not rush into his arms. Other than the first time he kissed her, and the second and the third, this was probably one of the most amazing moments in her life. After tonight, she would officially be engaged, and by October, only two months away, she would be Mrs. Hayley Beiler.

"You do know that you still have a choice right?" Duncan said much later, after they had finished dessert.

"I have made my choice, and it is to stay here with you," she said smiling.

They were seated on a wooden bench outside on the porch; waiting for the Lapp's to arrive.

"Are you a hundred percent sure?" he asked again, this time lacing his fingers with hers.

Hayley turned to him and placed her free hand over their entwined fingers. The past few months she had made the effort to learn their various customs, do bible study, get familiar with their laws, but she knew beyond anything that her life was here with him.

"Duncan, I am happy and I would not change this for anything," she said and then leaned close enough for her lips to brush his, "Ich liebe dich," she whispered and gave him a chaste kiss on his lips.

"And I love you, Hayley Jones," Duncan said, smiling from ear to ear and then quoted Songs of Solomon, "You are altogether beautiful, my darling, beautiful in every way."

~*~

Most of all, let love guide your way. Col 3:14

# SUNDAY

TILLIE TOLLIVER

**Chapter One**

The city roared on like a living beast below his apartment window.

Jason stared down through the night, watching thousands of cars navigate the streets of Tokyo like a light show. He took a sip of his soda, the ice clinking like chimes, and let the sound of the shower running, someone singing, drown out in the back of his mind. As his thoughts began to turn again, his pocket buzzed and started pouring out his ringtone.

Fumbling, he set down his glass and grabbed out his phone, briefly glancing at who was calling before he answered.

"Hey mom," he said softly, moving further into the room and away from the bathroom that was now billowing out steam.

Jason had moved away from home the second he was old enough to. His feet couldn't get far enough from the ground, his head was full of dreams of travel and living abroad.

He'd achieved that.

Japan was just the newest in a line of countries he'd called his home in the last few years. He'd learned a handful of languages, met hundreds and hundreds of amazing people. He had everything he wanted. His parents were the only piece in the puzzle that didn't quite fit.

"Jason, I thought you were going to call a couple hours ago?" his mom's voice was stern, yet worried. He was her only child, his parents had raised him with love and every hope that'd he'd always be a part of their lives, that didn't exactly pan out for them.

"Sorry mom, one of my coworkers wanted to get dinner and I forgot," he explained. The shower cut off in the next room, he didn't pay much attention to it.

"Another girlfriend?" his mom accused. Jason didn't want to lie to her, but he knew she wouldn't like the truth either.

"Mom, I'm allowed to make my own decisions," he said, sitting down in a soft arm chair next to the disheveled bed.

"Do any of your decisions have your father or me in mind?" she asked angrily. Jason held the phone to his ear with his shoulder as he poured more soda into his glass. "I haven't seen you in two years, your father doesn't think you're ever coming back," he could tell she was furious. "You're off contract until September, why don't you come home to us for a couple weeks? Why don't you want us to be part of your life?" she asked, she sounded so upset.

"I have a life here too, mom, and I want to be able to live it without you hovering," he said angrily. He was 25, hardly a child, he didn't need her to coddle him or treat him like one.

"How many countries have you lived in? How many girls have you made time in your life for? Yet you don't have time to come and see me or your father?" she asked angrily. "I love you Jason, we both love you so much, why do you put all of the work in this relationship on us?" she asked, almost crying. Jason felt bad, but he was hurt too.

"Why don't you just visit me then? Why do I have to change my life for you when you don't change at all for me?" he asked, angrily.

"We just want what's right for you," she replied, sobbing. Jason's stomach was in knots.

"Then maybe what's right for me is for you to let me make my own decisions," he said angrily.

"Jason!" his mother said, he could hear his father in the background asking what was wrong. Jason ended the call and set his phone down on the side table, shaken and upset.

He loved his parents, he honestly did.

He spent a lot of his early life with them as his best friends, wanting to spend every minute with them. He'd love sundays because they'd go to church as a family, and then a huge lunch with his grandparents as well. He knew that family was important.

He'd never forget those easy sundays, especially in the summer when the air was warm and yellow from the sun. Just his family and his friends, a couple boys and a beautiful blonde girl who was the pastor's daughters, they'd sit through the week's lessons together. Then his parents would tell him it was time to go, and although he'd miss the feeling of community he was happy to go with them.

He'd stopped going to church in his teen years.

He didn't think it was that important.

By the time he was 15 he realized that if he got a teaching degree he could go anywhere in the world he wanted to. All sorts of agencies at the time were advertising that you could teach abroad and they'd pay for your housing. He'd just have to get a two year degree (or less) and he could teach english and live basically anywhere.

He took to this immediately, and the moment he got his associates he was off.

He spent a year in south america, a couple in China, a year in South Korea, and now he was in Japan and loving it. The entire country was constantly moving and growing and changing and he loved it. He loved being able to see new things and people every day.

Sure, he'd dated several women along the way, but what was he supposed to do? Be alone for all of those years? He wanted to enjoy this life he'd made for himself.

He was finally doing something worthwhile, teaching and helping people grow. He felt so much satisfaction in his job and in his lifestyle, he didn't understand why his mom wanted him to go home so badly. He didn't understand why he felt so guilty about not going home.

He just wanted to be able to enjoy his life and his success.

The light switch clicked off in the bathroom, and out walked his coworker, turned girlfriend, Sara. She was graceful and beautiful, her sleek black hair was tied back into a ponytail.

"Who was on the phone?" she asked, picking her glasses up off a nightstand and sliding them on. He'd only started dating her because she showed interest in him. He wasn't sure if he even liked her, but she was beautiful. He felt the same about the city.

"My mom, she's missing me," he admitted.

"Did you tell her you've decided to start a new contract here?" she asked, digging through her purse for her phone.

"No, no need to upset her," he joked, he knew he'd upset her already. His mom was probably more than a little furious at him.

"I'm glad you chose to stay though, it'll be great to keep you another year," she said, smiling over at him. She clicked on her phone and started looking at any updates.

Jason smiled over at her and then stared back out the window at the night darkened city. He honestly didn't know what he wanted anymore.

Chapter Two

They were on their way out of Tokyo.

He'd rented a car for the day and they were going to go out of the city to the beaches, it had only been a handful of days since his mom called, but their conversation still weighed heavy on his heart.

"Would you hate me if I wanted to go back to the states for a week or two?" he asked her, glancing away from the road for just a moment. She creased her eyebrows and laughed.

"What do you mean? Of course not! Of course I wouldn't mind," she said while laughing. He was never completely sure where he stood with Sara.

That wasn't new for him.

None of the women he'd dated really left that strong of an impression.

He liked all of them, he knew that much. There was always that initial spark of interest, of desire, but he always found his mind wandering after a few weeks. He wasn't sure what was missing, what he wanted, but there was just something that wasn't quite right.

He didn't think he'd fallen in love with any of them.

He wanted to, he wanted that passion, that desire, that emotion that people write billions of stories and songs about. He just didn't think it had struck his heart yet. He thought that maybe it was his naivete kicking in, he was only 25, but all the same. He wanted a relationship where he felt as strongly for them as he felt for travel, as he felt for teaching.

His first girlfriend, a local from Guatemala while he was there, was a shop keep who helped him with his spanish, helped show him the country. She was sweet and creative, could paint like nobody's business, and she made sure that his life there was colorful and interesting. He thought it was love, until he realized that if he moved on to the next country, he could easily leave her behind and not feel terrible about leaving her.

He was completely sure that love was when you couldn't see yourself without someone.

After that the rest of the girls were all the same.

He'd meet a beautiful girl who was interesting, had a unique skill or interest, and he'd think 'finally, I've met the one'. Within weeks he'd catch himself staring out a window or getting bored around her, he'd try to fix his behavior, he'd never let them know what was wrong with him, but all the same he'd have to move on. He'd never met a girl who made him feel like he'd rather stay by her side than travel the world.

Sara was lovely, beautiful, clever, but she somehow wasn't what he needed either. She helped with scripting for video games in her free time when she wasn't teaching. She was able to show him parts of japan that tourists usually can't get close to, and yet he still felt this longing to move on. This feeling that something was missing.

The thought of going back home and staying there caught in his mind for the first time in a long time. He wanted to visit, but staying in the town where his parents lived, living a life like theirs, didn't appeal to him any more than his current one did.

He was losing passion, losing that need to travel, and he didn't think that small town would help at all.

The roads were busier that day.

Tokyo's roads are already a massive puzzle of bikes, motorcycles, cars, and pedestrians, but on busy days it could be horrifying. His brain felt the same, an immense puzzle that he wasn't even close to figuring out yet.

"Do you even like me?" Jason asked, frustrated with traffic and with his swirling feelings. Sara looked up from her phone, but didn't set it down. She was almost always connected to her phone, fingers tapping away and face alight with it's glow. If he'd liked her more he might have been jealous of it.

"Of course I do," she replied. "Why would you ask something like that?" she said, glancing back down at her phone.

"Would you want to come and meet my parents?" he asked, not sure even what he was doing at this point. She glanced up again from her screen.

"I think that's a bit much? I mean we're not that serious are we?" she asked, frowning slightly.

"Then what are we doing?" he asked, he looked over to her, away from the road.

"Enjoying our summer break off work," she replied, still confused. She obviously didn't want the same things from this as he did.

Jason was going to reply, was going to ask if she saw them going beyond this break, when a car sped through a red light and right into the door of Jason's side of the car.

It was all noise.

Sudden, loud, crushing noise as the world spun around the two of them and flipped their car onto it's side. Sara cried out, and the airbags deployed quickly, knocking them both against their seats with hot air and pressure. Jason was paralyzed with pain and fear, his whole body was buzzing in ache and adrenaline, and in moments he blacked out.

***

The smell that pulled him awake was of a lemony disinfectant. The distant beeping signifying his pulse was eager to try to lull him back to sleep, but the swimming pain that erupted from his arm as he shifted his weight stopped that from happening.

His eyes pulled open slowly like two lovers embracing, not eager to part. His head was throbbing with a migraine he wanted to sleep off. The room around him was bright, enveloping him him blue and white light, to compliment the white sheets and garb he was wearing. His neck creaked tiredly as he looked over to see why his right arm was aching, it was in a cast.

Panicking, he looked around, he couldn't remember, he didn't know why he was there. His left arm was wired up with an IV and a pulse-taker on his finger. He was alone in the room, save for the machines and a side table that had his phone and a jug of water and empty cup on it.

He heard a car honking outside the building, and the crash came flooding back to his mind, sending anxious chills down his body. He wiggled both of his feet and all of his toes, and watched their motions against the sheets. His right thigh ached, bruised, but he was alive, and mostly fine.

He felt lucky for getting out of that with just a broken arm. His phone caught his eye again and he stared it down.

He needed to call his mom and tell her what happened.

Slowly, he slid his wired arm over to his phone and picked it up, shaking as he turned it on and waited for the screen to load up. He started getting faint again, he was waiting too long and tired, and he started to pass out when he heard his mother's voice.

He was sure he hadn't called her.

He looked down at his phone and could see that there was no call made, and just when he was staring at it, confused, in she came.

His mother was a small woman, but had such a presence about her that you couldn't deny it.

"Jay you're awake!" she said, surprised and taken aback, she ran to his side and wrapped her warm and loving arms around him. "I was so terrified," she sobbed out, shaking. Jason breathed deeply, relaxed by her presence. "We could only afford the one ticket to get me out here," he said, letting him go and sobbing. She wiped her face with tissues from his nightstand. "Your father stayed behind but he loves you so much," she said, shaking her head.

"How long have I been here?" he asked, his voice cracked from lack of use. It surprised him.

"Almost three days," she said, flustered. "I found out about twelve hours after the accident, you were already out of surgery and I got the first ticket I could," she said, pulling a seat up to the side of his bed.

"Three days," he sighed out, horrified.

"You got the brunt of it, the girl riding with you got to just walk away with a couple scratches," she said.

Sara.

He forgot about Sara.

He was thankful she was alright, and felt immense guilt consume him for not remembering her until now.

"Has she been here to see me?" he asked, not sure what he was looking for.

"Not that I've seen, I've not left your side," his mother said apologetically.

It hurt, but not as bad as he knew it should have. He somehow always knew he was a temporary thing for her too. He took a sip of the water his mother poured for him, and sighed. If it wasn't for his mother he would have been completely alone in the hospital.

"I'm so sorry about our last call," she said softly, holding his hand gently. "If I had known," she paused, sucking in a breath. "If I had any clue that this could have happened I would have never-"

"Mom, it's okay, we both said harsh things, I'm sorry too," he said gently. She was really all he had anymore. She started crying again, he didn't know how to comfort her, but he knew what he needed to do all the same. "When is your flight back?" he asked, setting down his glass.

"Friday morning, it's Tuesday night right now," she answered. Jason nodded, and bit his lip thoughtfully.

"Alright, I'll fly back with you on Friday if I can get a seat," he said, nodding. His mother's eyes lit up so brightly she looked half her age.

"Jason! Really?" she asked, her eyes were filling with tears again.

"Just for a couple weeks, three at most, then I have to come back to teach," he explained, not wanting to get her hopes too high.

Chapter Three

The flight back was horribly long.

He hadn't been on a flight that long in years, and the fact that he was doing it while nursing a broken arm was even worse.

His mother had done most of his packing since he only had use of one arm. She'd also gotten them to the airport and fed him for the last couple days. She'd been a saint. She was on another section of the plane from him, so he didn't need to worry about squabbling. He tried to sleep, ate, listened to music, and tried to prepare himself as much as possible for a journey that he wasn't wanting to make.

When they landed he was greeted immediately by the immense heat of a North Carolina summer. The air felt different from Japan, it felt familiar and almost like home itself. He rolled his luggage behind him, and his mother chattered on about all of the people they'd have to see, all of the food she'd make.

He knew she was excited he was home for a bit, but he was exhausted.

His old room hadn't changed much in the last few years, his parents had made it into a guest room, but all of the furniture and books were still his. His eyes and heart traced over all of it with a loving nostalgia he hadn't felt for this home in years.

He unpacked some of his clothing (it's difficult to do when you've only got use of one arm), and went downstairs to look over the whole home. He'd spent his entire childhood there. They never moved, his parents had bought this home when they were his age, had him a couple years later. They were always so set in taking root.

He loved the home.

All of Saturday was a line of people stopping in to see him and welcome him back. He was always sure to say that it was a visit, but he wasn't sure that most of them believed him. Jason caught his mind tracing over their accents like familiar paths he'd once walked down, he could remember a time when he had that accent too. That southern drawl.

It had been replaced now, as with so many other things, with a more worldly take. His accent was just what could be deemed a 'plain american' accent. He didn't act or seem so southern anymore, he didn't seem like the same person he was growing up. Most of him was okay with that, but there was some small part that nagged him saying something was off, something was wrong.

He tried to push that part down under excitement of the thought of going back to Tokyo within a few weeks.

His father was happy to see him, he was sure, but showed it more in the way of patting the sofa next to him for Jason to sit down and watch tv with him.

One of the visitors was the pastor of the church he'd grown up going to.

Pastor James was about the same age as his parents, tall and intelligent. He'd spent a large part of his life travelling too, doing missionaries and helping where he could. His hand was large and warm as it shook Jason's and welcomed him back.

"Jason I hope to see you there for tomorrow's service," he said welcomingly, his smile was huge. Jason didn't have a chance to respond before the pastor was distracted by Jason's father mentioning an upcoming sport event.

Jason's mother, on the other hand, was smiling knowingly across the room.

He'd have to go to church after all.

***

Jason hadn't really packed anything that was appropriate for church.

He had a suit, but it wasn't that kind of church, it was comfortable, welcoming. He had jeans but that was a step too far in the other direction. It wasn't the kind of dressing up he was used to doing. Especially not with a cast on his arm.

There would be people he hadn't seen in over ten years there.

People who had no idea who he was anymore, just had their memories of him as a kid playing in the park next to the church.

He wasn't completely sure who he was anymore.

He walked downstairs and caught a glimpse of his father.

He sure as hell didn't want to be that.

Didn't want to be the old man who just sat on the couch all day and waited for another game or another movie. He wanted to be out in the world, taking in what sights and experiences he could.

His mother started hurrying them out the door.

They pulled up to the church just as a bunch of other people were filing out of their own.

Jason caught sight of Chuck, a friend he'd made in his childhood. He was getting ready to say hi to him when he saw Chuck was pulling a child's stroller out of the car and setting a baby in it.

It started to set in how long he'd been gone.

There were more than enough familiar faces, more than enough people who recognized him as well. It felt like some weird out-of-body experience. He'd seen so much and so many people, and now he was back where he'd grown up. Back on a summer sunday at the church he went to every weekend until he was a teenager.

He felt the years begin to slip away from him like heavy pieces of armor he'd build up by hand. He sang the hymns with the rest of the church, sat when he needed to, prayed when he needed to. It felt like a haze.

He didn't really have any clarity until near the end, when Pastor James stood at the front.

"We have a special treat today, my daughter Faye is here to sing for us, I'm really excited to hear what she's prepared," he said, grinning from ear to ear. A young woman with long pinned-back blonde hair and bright green eyes came up to the front.

Jason recognized her the moment he saw her.

Faye parted her lips and out came a beautiful and wordless song, peaking and dipping in ways that only birds had mastered before her.

Jason was mesmerized. He remembered when they were kids and would play together, how they'd spent so many years growing up together.

She was a beautiful woman now, looking more mature and grounded than he ever did.

Jason found himself on the edge of his seat the whole time she sang, when she finished her song he was disappointed, almost heartbroken. His mother had that smile on her face again, he didn't pay it any mind.

Chapter Four

"Faye, hey, wait up!" Jason said, jogging up to her. Church was let out and people were slowly crowding out to their cars to head out to lunch. Faye paused and turned to him, not recognizing him for a moment.

"Jason!" she exclaimed, surprised. She walked over quickly and hugged him tight.

"Ah- my arm," he tried to explain as he flinched from the pain.

"Oh, sorry about that," she laughed. Her accent was strong like the others, but something was just golden about her, besides just her hair. "I heard you were back in town, I didn't expect you to show up here though," she said, leaning against her car. Her white and yellow dress flit softly in the sweet summer breeze.

"Yeah, your dad talked me into it," he said, laughing a little. "You've kept up singing?" he asked, relaxing a little.

"I did, but now I'm also a veterinarian," she explained. She was beautiful. Jason felt his heart reaching out to her in ways it hadn't for anyone else before.

"Do you still live in the area?" he asked.

"Yep, just over near the old cotton farm on Red Street," she said. He was relieved and wasn't quite sure why.

"Do you want to catch a meal or something while I'm here to catch up?" he asked, pulling out his phone. Faye's lips crinkled into a smile and she nodded.

"I'd like that a lot."

***

Getting ready for a date was more stressful than ever. He wore dark jeans and a button up that would fit his cast with the sleeve buttons undone. His mom tried to convince him to get a haircut, but he didn't want to look like he was trying too hard.

They were just going to pick up some food and either go to a movie or hang out at the old bowling alley that had been there since before they were born.

When he took his dad's car to pick her up, it felt like high school.

She came out wearing a black and white dress with a small cardigan, she looked like a model, like someone far too spectacular to still be kicking around in this small town.

He kept that thought to himself.

They went to a pizza restaurant and he tried to think about things he could talk about without seeming like a tool. They ended up discussing where they've been and what they'd been doing for so many years. She'd lived an amazing life, getting to be a veterinarian and help her father with the church. She even recorded an album with one song that got played nationally.

She wanted to be a vet, not a singer, though. It's what she'd always wanted.

Jason wasn't sure anymore about what he'd always wanted. As they left for the bowling alley, he began to think that it might be her.

They ended up going to a movie, a remake of something that had been released in the 80s, and he held her hand a little at the end of it.

He wasn't sure what he was feeling.

He wasn't sure what he was doing.

Jason knew he was going back to Japan in just a couple weeks, and somehow he was feeling conflicted about traveling for the first time in his entire life.

He had to be honest with her.

He wasn't sure how.

"Faye," he started. They were walking back to the car. The sky was lit brightly with stars and a half moon, crickets and other critters filled the air with their songs in the breeze. "I have another contract coming up where I could be starting another year in Japan," he explained. They stopped walking, her fingertips slipped out of his.

"Wait, I thought you were here to stay?" she asked, confused. He hated this. Jason could feel his heart drop into his stomach.

"I mean, that's what everyone's saying, but I have to get back on that plane in a couple weeks and fly back, I even told your dad that," he explained.

"Why didn't you tell me, then?" she asked. Faye was visibly hurt, this shook Jason.

"I," he stumbled with his words. "I don't know, I was really excited to see you again," he tried to explain.

"I'm not here to be a passing fancy like any girl you've dated while hopping countries, Jason, I'm not like that," there were tears in her eyes, Jason hated himself.

"I know, I'm sorry, that's why I'm letting you know," he explained.

"You're cruel Jason, cruel," she said, shaking her head and starting to cry. "Please drive me home, I think we're done here," she said, upset. She wiped her face and headed to the car.

Jason didn't know what to do, didn't know what to say.

He'd never felt like this before saying goodbye. It was like nausea and panic mixed together.

He did as she asked, though, and when they pulled up to her house she got out without a word and walked into her home.

Jason watched her, angry at himself, angry at the situation.

Chapter Five

The next week was miserable.

Jason's cast had begun to be itchy, he was restless and depressed. He overheard his mother telling his father she was worried about him.

He could understand why.

He didn't eat much at all, didn't do much besides watch television or go on his computer. He didn't go to church with them the following sunday.

Jason was sitting in the back yard reading one of his childhood books when his father came up to him. It was nearly evening, the sun was setting a golden pink hue over the sky and town. His father sat down next to him and stared off at the grass ahead of them.

"Son, what's going on?" he asked, scratching his beard a little. Jason set down his book and sighed.

"I don't know, I think I miss Tokyo," he lied, stretching a little. His father grunted, and he knew that wasn't going to be a good enough answer. "I don't know what I want right now and it's bugging me because I hurt Faye," he let out. It was honest, even if it soured his tongue as it passed over it. His father glanced over at him and nodded understandingly.

"Have you talked to her?" his dad asked. Squirrels were chattering in the tree nearby.

"No, I don't see the point in that, I'm leaving," Jason explained, upset. "Why let her get her hopes up when I'm probably just going to fly off next week?"

"Probably?" his dad asked, surprised. Jason bit the inside of his cheek, unsure why he said that.

"I don't know," Jason said. "I haven't felt like this about anybody, I can't stop thinking about her," Jason explained. He was 25, he thought he'd run out of things to be surprised by.

"Sounds like you should talk to her, tell her how you feel," his father explained.

"What's the point in that? I'm leaving," Jason said uncomfortably.

"Probably."

Jason stared down at his own hands.

"There's a week left, say what you need to and see if it changes anything," his father said, stretching.

"Alright," Jason said, sick at even the thought of it.

***

Jason texted Faye after dinner that night.

"Can I see you this week? I really want to talk to you about something," he typed, not sure what to say. The second he clicked send, he laid back on his bed, the bed he grew up sleeping in. The home he spent his entire adolescent life.

What the hell was he going to tell her.

He couldn't just flat out say that he felt like he might be in love with her. Was he in love with her? Is this what he wanted? He didn't know, he wasn't sure. All he knew was that when he thought about her he felt different, he wanted different things. He liked who he could be with her.

He wasn't sure if that meant staying here, or asking her to move there. Hell, how would he ask her to move there? What could he say that would make her want to make a huge move like that? They just started talking again a short while ago.

No amount of childhood comradery would make up for not seeing someone for ten years.

What if she didn't reply?

He stared over at his phone, it had only been minutes but they had dragged by like frozen concrete.

He didn't know what he wanted.

How could he possibly ask her to decide anything?

Tired, he went to bed for the night and tried not to be kept awake by his worries.

***

When he woke up the next morning his phone battery was dead. Pessimistic and craving breakfast, he plugged it in and trudged downstairs to make himself some eggs.

He was sure she wouldn't respond.

He was sure she was done with him.

When he went back up after breakfast his phone was blinking out a text from 8:45 am.

"Sure, how about lunch today at noon? At The Biscuit Bag," it said brightly.

His phone said it was 11:05.

"Crap," he said, rushing to text her back a quick 'alright' before jumping into the shower. She wanted to see him! She was going to give him a second chance! He should have waited for his phone instead of being a coward, but he still had an opportunity.

He was luckily so rushed to get ready and get there that by the time he arrived he realized he hadn't stressed once about what to say. At 11:58 he pulled into the lot of the restaurant and saw her leaning against her car, her bright green eyes watched some birds in a nearby tree.

"Faye," he said as he closed his car door and jogged over to her.

"Heya," she replied, obviously a little uncomfortable.

"I wanted to let you know-"

"Let's go order some food first, I'm starving," she cut him off. He wasn't hungry at all, but he agreed and ordered a milkshake and order of fried okra.

When they were settled at the table his nerves set back in, but he pushed them aside.

"I want the chance to date you," he said as she took a sip of her orange cola. She raised her eyebrows at him.

"I'm not moving to Japan for someone I hardly know right now," she said, laying it flat out. Jason didn't care, as he realized it he felt amazing.

"I want to stay here, if that means I can date you. I've never felt like this about anyone, but I want to ask before I change my plans," he explained. She paused for a moment before replying.

"I like you a lot too, to be honest," she admitted. "I have thought about you a lot for the last couple weeks, why didn't you show up to church? I was going to talk to you, but," her voice drifted off. She bit her lower lip. Jason felt like he had won every lottery ever, she felt the same.

They finished their lunch over pleasant chatter. He felt so comfortable and happy with her, so right. He paid the bill and they headed out to the parking lot.

"Can I kiss you," he asked softly, brushing some of her hair away from her face.

"Please," she said, smiling. His hand slid down to her cheek and they kissed softly, it was electric and buzzing and Jason hadn't ever felt this way. He honestly hadn't. It was just a kiss but it felt like every fiber of his being was slowly unravelling, and he was just his lips. Just the parts of his body that were in contact with her.

When they parted her face was flushed and she slowly opened her eyes.

"I guess I'll be sticking around then," he said gently, quirking his lips into a smile.

"Only if you promise to go to church with me every Sunday," she said softly.

"For you I'd go to church every single day," he teased. Faye laughed and they kissed again.

This was everything he ever needed.

# REDEEMABLE

RICKI CROSS

<u>**Upstate**</u>

He knew what it was before the courier got out of the van. Even the neighbors peering from their windows like buzzards for the carcass could detect the scent of complete annihilation. As the heavyset messenger lumbered up the snow-lined driveway and met him on the front steps, Patrick felt the sick sensation of defeat in his stomach and without a word, held out his hand to accept the manila envelope the man in the khaki uniform was handing him.

"Are you Reverend Patrick Dean?" the carrier asked. Swallowing the lump in his throat, Patrick nodded. "I need you to sign this, Mr. Dean. You've been served."

Without argument, Patrick took the pen and scribbled his name before retreating quickly into the house with the package before the tears flowed from his burning eyes. He leaned heavily against the door and exhaled slowly, trying to collect himself. Then, he moved to the staircase and sat down. With trembling hands, he tore open the envelope and read the dreaded contents. Cynthia had filed for a divorce. A divorce. The word reverberated through his skull like a bullet. Of course he had been expecting it but the reality was still almost too much for him to stomach.

Unsteadily, he rose to his feet. He tried to remember the last time he had eaten. He couldn't recall his last meal. That was probably a bad sign. He wiped his tired, streaked eyes and walked into the kitchen, determined to reclaim some of his former strength. His life may have been falling apart but he was still a strong man, a man of God and God would want him to live and fight another day. *God wouldn't want you divorcing your wife,* a snide voice in his ear whispered. Patrick shoved the thought out of his head and yanked open the fridge with too much force. A glass ketchup bottle fell to the floor and shattered. Jamba came running eagerly into the room, smelling food like the little scavenger she was.

"No! Get out of here before you cut your paw!" he commanded the bloodhound. She paused uncertainly and slowly backed away, giving him a hurt look. As he quickly cleaned up the mess, he realized that the ketchup he had just disposed of was just about the last staple of food left in his refrigerator. A scan of the pantry produced the same results. He needed to go shopping. He had been to the grocery store once since Cynthia had left almost three weeks prior. Shuffling into the hall, he ushered Jamba up the stairs and changed out of his robe into a pair of raggedy track pants and old sweatshirt. The dog looked up at him expectantly, her tail wagging. Patrick was overcome by guilt. When was the last time he had taken the pooch on a decent walk? He vowed he would do that when he got back from the store. He scratched her ears affectionately and grabbed his keys off the dresser, purposely avoiding the reflection in the mirror. He knew what it would show; a man riddled with shame and anguish.

Thankfully the snow had stopped falling during the night and only the white mounds piled on the side of the road were reminiscent of the two-day storm that had finally ended. As Patrick pulled into the small parking lot of the local grocer, he was relieved to find it almost deserted. It was a Tuesday morning after all. Hurriedly, he slipped inside and pulled a cart into the produce section. Without much regard for what he was selecting, he began throwing items in, hoping to be in and out before the inevitable occurred. Yet, as he rounded the corner into the condiment aisle, he almost collided with a young boy who was crouched near the floor, peering at the pickles with intense scrutiny. The child looked up at him, startled and then his serious expression melted into a huge smile.

"Pastor Pat!" he yelled. Patrick cringed, feeling the blood drain from his face. The boy ran over and threw his arms around the older man. Patrick gently hugged young Austin back and released him, looking around for his mother. As if on cue, she came storming up the lane and seized her son's hand, glaring viciously at Patrick.

"Pastor Pat where have you been? We keep looking for you at church but you don't go up on stage and talk anymore!"

"No, Austin, I don't do sermons at the church anymore," Patrick said quietly, averting his eyes from the woman's steely gaze.

"Oh! Why not? I like it when you tell the stories about the animals and the boat and the snake and the giant. The other Pastor is no fun. He just reads pages out of this big boring book." If Patrick hadn't been so depressed, he would have chuckled at the five-year old's interpretations.

"You should give Pastor Michael a chance, Austin. He is a very nice man," Patrick chided, chucking the child under his chin.

"More importantly, son, he is not a drunk, an adulterer or a sinner," Austin's mother chimed, pulling her son from Patrick's reach. Both Austin and Patrick blinked at her tone. Patrick's face turned crimson and as he excused himself, he heard Austin say, "Mom, what's a dalter?"

Somehow, Patrick managed to purchase the few objects he had tossed into the cart and make it home in a fog. When Jamba greeting him at the door, he completely forsook his promise to take her for a walk and after haphazardly throwing the groceries into the kitchen, he threw himself onto his bed and stared hopelessly up at the ceiling. *I am a pariah. This will haunt me for the rest of my life. I need to get out of here.* There was something cold and wet on his hand. Jamba had followed him into the room and was nuzzling his hand with a cold nose. He petted her head absently and as he sat up, his eyes fell onto a worn photograph on the dresser. Slowly, he rose to his feet and picked up the picture. While the frame had been there for as long as he could remember, he hadn't heeded its existence in years. Gently, he wiped the dust off the silver and smiled wistfully at his own happy expression in the image. He had been so young, holding a fishing pole and grinning without a care in the world. But it was the property in the background which held his attention. Patrick knew where he had to go.

**Down South**

It was just as dirty and dilapidated as he remembered. There were even more holes in the roof than the last time he had visited and at least one hurricane had eaten away at most of the siding. Thankfully, the cabin was miniscule enough that the contractor with whom he had spoken guaranteed a full repair in about a week but until then, Patrick and Jamba were going to be contending with the elements.

As man and dog slowly ascended the rickety steps, under the humble cypress trees, some feral animal mewled angrily and hissed from under the slats in the porch. Jamba yelped in fear but Patrick was overwhelmed with nostalgia of childhood. This cottage had been in his family for four generations. His great grandparents had built it and birthed all twelve of their children within its five rooms. His father had been born there, along with six of his aunts. After that era, the place had been used strictly as a getaway property for the cousins but as everyone aged and became successful, the majority of the family had left the deep south and ventured onto "better" things. Suddenly everyone had cabins in Aspen or summer homes in the Hamptons. It seemed that Patrick was apparently to only one who felt a kinship to the rundown house, despite its sorry state. Granted, he didn't spend the time he wanted in the bayou but he had always had a great affection for the property and its history.

The door was not locked and Patrick rolled his suitcase into the tiny front room which was both the kitchen and living room. Grandpa's antique rocker was still there and while there were spider webs in every corner, the potbelly stove was where he remembered, the tiny bar fridge was in the kitchen and even the wash basin was by the back door. *If this were the city, there would be nothing left. Someone would have stolen all the belongings and some squatters would be living in attic.* But this was not the city. This was the serene, trusting south where things were still sacred and people watched out for one another. He reached out and flicked a light switch but of course there was no electricity. He would have to tend to that tomorrow. Beside him, Jamba whined again. She was out of her element but the truth was, the reason Patrick had rescued her from the shelter was that she reminded him of one of his grandpa's hunting hounds. He had even named her Jamba for Jambalaya despite Cynthia's protests.

"What an awful name for a dog! It's bad enough that she's so ugly! Take her back and get something smaller and cuter, Pat!" Yet the dog had stuck and so had the name and it had truly been the only reminder Patrick had of his childhood in the womb of America. From under the rocker, a scared green snake slithered out and disappeared into a crack in the slat floor. Jamba howled and ran out of the still open screen door.

"Jamba!" Patrick dropped his suitcase and tore after her down the dirt road. He caught glimpse of her tail disappear around the corner and he rushed toward the bushes. Panting, he turned around the bend and stopped abruptly. Jamba was in the arms of a boy of maybe eight, shivering in fright. But behind the child and dog was a woman standing in the doorway of her cottage. Patrick could make out the tall outline of a black haired woman in a blue dress but he could not see her face. Even so, she took his breath away – or at least the little breath he had left after chasing his hound.

"Jamba! Come!" Patrick found his voice. Reluctantly, the dog slunk out of the boy's lap and retreated to his master. The woman stepped out of the home and Patrick's heart leapt into his throat as the beauty of her face enthralled him. She had big blue eyes filled with wisdom and compassion, a lovely cream complexion and a welcoming smile.

"I'm so sorry! She got frightened off by a snake. She's never seen one before," Patrick heard himself babble. The woman's smile widened.

"Well I understand that," she replied with a sweet Southern drawl which only enhanced her attractiveness. "She ain't hurting nobody ova here. Damien 'n I love dogs, don't we, honey?"

The young boy nodded eagerly, dark eyes wide but his lips did not move. The woman continued forward. She wiped her hands on the apron covering the skirt of her dress and offered a palm to Patrick. He accepted it and noticed how soft were her hands.

"Sarah Jane," she said. "An' this is ma son, Damien. Y'all ain't from around here. I kin tell."

Patrick shook his head.

"I'm Patrick. This is Jamba. We're from...out of town." Patrick was reluctant to give her too much information. The idea was to retreat from people, not make new friends to disappoint.

"We jus' moved here from Baton Rouge 'bout a year ago. Where y'all stayin'?" Patrick pointed down the road.

"In the Dean's place. It's my family's but no one much uses it anymore." Sarah Jane raised an eyebrow in surprise.

"Y'all can't stay there! All them 'coons and cats be livin' up in there now. It ain't safe nor sanitary!"

"I have contractors coming to fix it up. We won't be like this too long," Patrick assured her. He suddenly noticed Damien staring intently at him.

"How old are you, Damien?" Patrick asked. He had always liked children and they seemed to feel the same about him. The boy did not answer but he did not look away.

"Damien don't talk much," Sarah Jane said quietly. Patrick nodded understandingly. He smiled at the boy.

"Nothing wrong with that," he replied. "Still waters always run the deepest."

A look of surprise and appreciation flashed through Sarah Jane's lovely eyes.

"Why don't y'all get settled in and come back fer dinner. Y'all like gumbo? Ma pa always said I make the best gumbo this side of New Orleans."

"If it's all right with your husband. I wouldn't want to impose." Patrick almost choked on the word "husband." He had no idea what had come over him. He never had attractions like this to perfect strangers but for some reason he was drawn to this woman. *You need to walk away before you get yourself in even more trouble,* he warned himself. But his own warning went unheeded. Sarah Jane laughed throatily.

"If y'all kin find him, y'all kin ask him yourself," she chuckled. "We ain't seen Damien's pa since the boy was knee high to a grasshopper." Patrick wasn't sure if he was contrite or relieved. Probably a bit of both. "Y'all come at 6. Bring yer Jamba. I'll have a bowl fer her too."

Back at the shack, Patrick perched gently on his grandpa's rocker and began to sway back and forth. He was thinking about Sarah Jane and the sense that he had known her for a long while. He wondered if her black waves were as soft as they appeared. Guiltily, he tried to shift his thoughts but he couldn't seem to get her smile out of his head with the slight gap between her teeth and the endearing but almost inaudible lisp her mouth produced. Her eyes reminded him of someone...abruptly, Patrick sat up in the wooden chair, startling Jamba from her sleeping position at his feet. Shame stained his cheeks a scarlet he feared would never fade. He realized exactly why he found Sarah Jane so desirable; she was a physical combination of his wife and the woman with whom he had ruined the sanctity of his marriage.

### <u>Upstate</u>

### *<u>One Month Prior</u>*

*"I really have no interest in going, Cyndi," Patrick sighed as he finished tying his tie in the full length mirror. "I don't see why I need to be there."*

*"Oh Pat, you're marrying them next week. Just go, have a scotch, make a toast and come home. It's your duty to attend these events." Patrick sighed again and turned to face his wife, feeling a slight sense of jealousy. She was already in her pajamas, curled up in bed with her knitting. He knew she was right. Bachelor parties were a rite of passage and he was hosting the ceremony for the happy couple but he had never been a fan of the ritual. He was always secretly relieved when the grooms planned rowdy*

*gatherings and opted to leave him out of them. He would much rather be home playing ball with Jamba or reading a book.*

*Dutifully, he dropped a kiss on Cynthia's cheek and headed out of the bedroom.*

*"Please don't forget to let Jamba out before you go to bed."*

*"You don't need to remind me every time you leave the house, Pat. I'll let her out." Patrick paused at the doorway and looked back at his other half. She was still a lovely woman, even after fifteen years of marriage. Her honey blonde hair was always well coifed, her nails perfectly manicured and she had vivid, intelligent blue eyes which he had initially fallen in love with what seemed like a million years ago. Even ready for bed, she had a cold cream mask on her face and curlers in her hair in preparation for tomorrow.*

*"Cynthia, please don't neglect Jamba. She is getting older and her bladder can't handle holding it for long periods of time." Cynthia dropped the scarf she was working on and glared at him.*

*"Are you suggesting that I don't take care of your stupid dog? I always let her out, Patrick!"*

*Patrick held his ground.*

*"Last week when I came home from my conference, she had peed on the welcome rug. She never does anything like that unless she hasn't been out. I'm just asking you to remember, that's all." Cynthia sat forward rigidly in the bed, incensed.*

*"Well maybe something's wrong with her because I'm always letting her out when you're away. And if you don't trust me to do it, then hire someone to do it for you, you ungrateful boor! I take darn good care of that useless animal even though I didn't want her. But you didn't seem to care and brought her home anyway. Now I'm not babysitting properly for you. You are insufferable, Patrick. You better go before I say something I regret." Biting his lip, Patrick heeded her advice and left the house, fuming.*

*He was at the venue housing the bachelor party in fifteen minutes. The groomsmen had chosen a quaint lakeside tavern for the party. It promised* to be low key and well behaved but Patrick was still shaking with anger when he walked inside. He tried to stuff his emotions under a superficial smile and greeted the other party goers. But he couldn't get to the bar fast enough where he ordered his first scotch.

Two hours had gone by and Patrick had really no recount of where the time had escaped but around ten thirty p.m. he was chatting to a mysterious sloe eyed beauty in a dimly lit corner of the restaurant. Her luxuriant black hair caught the candlelight like magic flecks and while later Patrick could not recall what they had discussed, he remembered wanting to hear her speak so he could listen to her mellifluous, throaty voice. An hour later, the groom had approached him to gently question how he was getting home and Patrick was apparently sitting very close to the ethereal beauty in the booth, still drinking scotch (at least he was told the following day).

By this point he had turned off his phone to avoid Cynthia's texts and phone calls.

Midnight found Patrick with the exotic stranger in the bathroom in a very compromising position. Two of the groomsmen had walked in on the act and quickly exited, waiting for Patrick to come out of the washroom so they could drive him home. He was barely coherent from the amount of alcohol he had consumed. They quietly unlocked his front door and gently pushed him into the house, awkwardly dressed and falling down. Neither of the men had wanted to explain to Mrs. Dean how her husband had come to be in such a state or be forced to answer any questions. The only certainty Patrick had at that point was that Jamba had not been let out for she urinated all over his feet as soon as he stumbled into the house.

The following morning, the entire town's phone lines were afire. It was too juicy a scandal to ignore. Pastor Pat was drunk and cheating on his wife with a stranger in front of members of his own parish? He was an instant outcast. He didn't even have time to beg Cynthia for forgiveness. By the time he had slept off the alcohol, he was staring at her emptied closet and dresser drawers.

## Down South

Patrick snapped out of his reverie of mortification and glanced at his watch. Sarah Jane would be expecting him and Jamba very shortly.

"Come on, girl," he said to the pooch and they hurried out of the cottage down the road. As they neared the bushes, Patrick heard screaming. He and Jamba paused mid-step and listened. The shrieking continued from Sarah Jane's house. He began to run toward the commotion. Tearing around the corner, there was a crash and Damien threw open the screen and took off like the devil himself was on his heels. Tears streaked his face and he was wailing high and feral but he had disappeared before Patrick could react. When he looked back at the house, Sarah Jane stood on the threshold looking defeated. She tried to force a smile as she saw him but failed. Tears misted her incredible eyes as she waved for them to enter.

"I'm sorry y'all had to see that," she said, tiredly as she shooed them into her small home. "Damien has good days and bad ones. This ain't been the best one."

"We can do this another day. Please go deal with your son," Patrick said, gently. Sarah Jane shook her head.

"Oh no! I been slavin' away over a hot stove all day. Y'all gonna stay and eat. Damien will be back when he calms down some. Dontcha worry. It happens all the time. It's one of the reasons I decided to move all the way out ta here. Ain't no one to witness his breakdowns. In Baton Rouge, ma neighbors done be callin' the police an' Child Services on me once a week. No one understands what it's like." Her normally bright eyes were clouded with sadness.

"If you don't mind me asking, have you taken him to a doctor?"

Sarah Jane gestured for him to sit down at a modest kitchen table done in solid pine. She laughed mirthlessly.

"Yessir. An' all of them want to put him on this drug an' that drug. I even had him try some of them. Turned him into a zombie or robot or somethin'. Ain't no way for a child to live. So I keep him home an' school him here but I ain't the most educated woman but when I think of the alternative, I might as well lock him up in an asylum." She choked on her last words and sobbed. Her hand flew to her mouth as she tried to stifle the raw emotion she was feeling. Patrick was instantly at her side, embracing her. She stiffened at his unexpected touch and he backed away immediately.

"Oh, I'm so sorry! I didn't mean to – "

"No no! It ain't you, Patrick. It's...I ain't really had much male companionship since Damien's daddy up and left. I know you were just bein' supportive. I'm sorry I'm such poor company." They grinned sheepishly at one another and sat at the table.

"The gumbo's just simmerin'. Would you like a beer or glass of wine? Actually, I think I even have some of ma pa's moonshine in the cellar." Patrick shook his head quickly.

"No, no thank you. Just water will be fine." Sarah Jane's smile widened further.

"Not much of a drinkin' man?" she asked as she went to the small fridge and retrieved a pitcher of lemon water.

"No," he replied simply.


## Upstate

### *One Year Prior*

*"That was a wonderful service, Pastor Pat! I hope you and Cynthia will join us for brunch today" The Bransons were smiling hopefully at him and his instinct was to decline but Cynthia was pinching his arm ruthlessly.*

*"We would be honored to join you, Joe! Thank you so much for your continued support and Lana, your brownies were the biggest hit at the bake sale yesterday! I think you singlehandedly made our goal happen!" Cynthia cut in, beaming. "What can we bring?"*

*The couple and Cynthia continued to chat and Patrick wandered off toward the playground. The Bransons had invited them to brunch every single Sunday since Patrick had become Pastor and he had always managed to avoid their invites.*

*"It's awful manners, Patrick! You must think of what the members of this parish do for our church. Next time they ask us, you better accept!" Cynthia had warned him just before the service that morning. Patrick had merely nodded but he had no intention of doing what she suggested. Of course Cynthia knew that and had made it a point to be at his side afterward. He was beginning to find himself irritated with his wife over the tiniest issues. But he had found a way to cope with her annoying habits. As he watched the children playing happily on the monkey bars, he forced his mind out of the spot where it always went and circled back to the rear entrance of the church. The fire door was open and he slipped inside, unnoticed. He made his way to his office and secured the door behind him. Then he dropped tiredly into the high back leather chair and unlocked the bottom drawer to his desk. He pulled open the mickey of vodka and took a huge swig. He paused for a moment and after the burning sensation in his throat passed, he helped himself to one more before replacing the bottle and popping cough drop into his mouth. Well at least there would be mimosas at brunch.*

## Down South

Sarah Jane had not exaggerated her culinary talents; the gumbo was phenomenal. She had even set up a bowl for Jamba which the dog inhaled in three bites and begged for seconds. As Sarah Jane had anticipated, Damien did reappear before dinner was through. He ignored both of the adults and sat on the floor to play with Jamba who relished the attention.

"So do ya do fer a livin', Patrick?" Sarah Jane inevitably asked. Patrick considered lying but there was something about this woman that made him want to only speak in truths.

"I was a pastor but I'm not really doing anything at the moment," he responded, looking down at his bowl. Sarah Jane's face seemed to light up like a Christmas tree.

"Y'all must be really smart then!" she exclaimed. Patrick laughed.

"Well I wouldn't go that far!"

"Y'all gone to college, ain't ya?" Patrick nodded.

"Would y'all be willin' ta help me with schoolin' Damien? I ain't so good in English an' history an' artsy stuff. I kin hold ma own in math and science but spellin' dang if I don't go messin' everythin' up!" Patrick was taken aback by the offer.

"Well, I…"

"Oh, I kin pay ya! I'm a researcher actually. I do online consultin' for some huge firms so money ain't really a problem."

"I would be happy to help you with Damien," Patrick responded. "If Damien would be willing to have me. Damien, would you mind if I come and help with some of your lessons?"

The child looked completely startled at being addressed. He stared at Patrick with hole boring black eyes and then, after what seemed like an eternity, he shrugged, barely nodded and turned back to Jamba.

"Well I guess it's settled then! When do we start?"

The following morning, Patrick woke to contractors on the roof. The pale morning light was sparkling through the trees and despite his sore back from sleeping on the rough wood pallet in one of the two bedrooms, he felt elated for the first time in as long as he could remember. Even Jamba seemed contented as she followed him to the outhouse. He walked down toward the water, keeping a watchful eye out for alligators and splashed some cool water on his face before retreating back to the cottage. He dug a pair of jeans and a t-shirt out of the suitcase and quickly changed before leaving the construction crew and heading to meet Sarah Jane and Damien. He thought about the developmentally challenged little boy and wondered about Sarah Jane's husband. He wondered if a father would have changed the child's life substantially. He angrily pondered what kind of man would abandon a boy who needed more support than the average child and leave the mother alone to contend with the aftermath. Then he thought about Cynthia.

### <u>Upstate</u>
### *<u>Fifteen Years Prior</u>*

*"Are you happy, Patrick?" she asked as they drove home from the cabin. She seemed annoyed at having spent part of their honeymoon in the swamp but she didn't say anything out loud.*

*"Of course I'm happy! I've married my queen, we're starting our lives together upstate where we'll have a gaggle of babies and we are going to live happily ever after! How could I be anything but ecstatic? How about you? Any regrets yet?" He grinned teasingly at her and Cynthia flashed him a brief smile.*

*"Of course I am!" She turned to watch the gorgeous scenery. "Patrick?"*

*"Yes, my love?"*

*"I need to tell you something."*

*"You can tell me anything. I am your husband." He grinned wider as he said the word. He loved the way it sounded. "Husband. I like the sound of that. I wonder if I'm going to like the sound of 'daddy' as much. Probably. I guess we'll find out."*

*"Patrick, I had an accident when I was young, I fell off a horse," Cynthia said quietly. "And the doctor's have told me that I can't have children."*

### *<u>Ten Years Prior</u>*

*His head was pounding. He hadn't had a migraine since his late teens but the air pressure was affecting his blood pressure and he was suffering terribly.*

*"Cyndi? Cynthia?" he croaked from the bedroom but there was no answer. Only Jamba lay on the pillow beside him, nuzzling his neck. "Cyndi?"*

*She must have gone out while I was sleeping, he thought. The thought of getting out of the bed was agonizing but he had no choice. He slowly and painfully rose to his feet, trying to move as gingerly as possibly. The nausea was overwhelming but he needed to take some Aspirin before the pain got much worse or else he would end up hospitalized. Slowly, he shuffled into the bathroom and tried to remember where Cynthia kept the pain medication. He was unaccustomed to taking any form of medicine. He began rummaging through drawers when the cabinet in the bathroom produced no results. He found himself in Cynthia's beauty products when his hand closed around a circular package. When he looked down at it, he thought the pain had affected his vision but the logical, educated side of him knew what he was staring at birth control pills. His wife had been taking birth control pills.*

### *Five Years Prior*

*The party was in full swing and while everyone was having a grand old time, Patrick had one of his now trademark headaches. He looked around everywhere for Cynthia but he couldn't find her. Finally, he escaped to the backyard for some fresh air and snuck around to the side of the house. What he saw made his blood run cold; Cynthia was passionately kissing a man he considered to be one of his best friends. And Patrick slowly backed away and never mentioned the scene to anyone.*


### Down South

When Patrick appeared at the door, Damien actually smiled at him for the first time and he felt his heart swell. He realized that the child was more likely smiling at Jamba but Patrick still took it as a positive sign. The boy allowed them into the house and led them to a sunroom in the rear of the house. Sarah Jane was waiting for them there with coffee and fresh fruit for breakfast. The room was designed to be an educational but stimulating environment. The windows overlooked the bayou and all of the day creatures were peeking out of their hiding spots for the day. A black and white board were set up as to not obstruct the stunning view. Sarah Jane had already laid out the lessons for the day and Damien took his seat in an old style school desk. They started with a basic math lesson and Patrick was pleased to see how quickly Damien finished his assignments. The child had a natural knack for math and science. *Just like his mother*, Patrick thought with appreciation. He was warmed as he saw the interaction between mother and son. While Damien was non-verbal, the managed to communicate through gestures and he genuinely seemed to hang on to her every word. When it came Patrick's time to take stage, he began with one of his sermons, one that young Austin had liked so much, David and Goliath. He noted happily that Damien was enraptured by the story and afterward they took a break for lunch.

Damien took his tuna fish sandwiches outside to share with Jamba while Sarah Jane and Patrick sat in the cozy kitchen and talked. To Patrick's surprise, he found himself opening up to her about Cynthia, things he had never shared with anyone. She in turn talked about Damien's father and they both felt a deep connection to one another through the strangers they had married. They talked about their spouses openly.

"Damien's daddy was neva any good at facin' problems," Sarah Jane said. "I guess I shoulda seen that before we got hitched. He drank like a fish and got inta all kinds of bar fights but I was all struck by them big ole black eyes and them pretty white teeth. As soon as he realized Damien wasn't like other boys, he hightailed it outta town lickity split. Neva heard a word from him in ova five years now. Ain't no big loss. Damien an' I always did okay together."

"Even after I discovered that Cynthia had been lying to me on so many levels, I still wanted to be a good husband to her. I really did love her. Or at least the woman I believed she was. Aside from that one horrible, stupid night, I was never unfaithful to her. I never even considered it."

They smiled at each other and Patrick reached across the table to put his hand over hers.

"We do the best we can given what we got," Sarah Jane told him, giving his palm a gentle squeeze.

"And remember that God won't ever throw anything at us we can't handle," Patrick replied.

The days were long and wonderful, filled with lessons for Damien and walks through the swampland. The contractors finished the cabin and there was finally a bathroom, electricity and running water within its walls. Even Jamba was thriving in her new environment, attempting to befriend the racoons and once even a gator. The nights were less and less lonely, spent playing Monopoly with Damien and Sarah Jane. When the boy would go to bed, Sarah Jane and Patrick would talk until the wee hours of the morning, listening to the fish splashing in the water and the crickets chirping. They never seemed to run out of subjects to discuss. Sarah Jane was worldly and intelligent and a wonderful conversationalist. Once in a while they would drive into town and see a film at the small outdoor theater or go for ice cream. Sarah Jane and Patrick would stroll arm in arm and sometimes, Patrick would feel a small hand slip into his for a moment or two and then Damien would run off to be with Jamba.

One morning, a courier pulled up on the dirt road outside of the cabin just as Patrick was leaving for Sarah Jane's house. His heart in his throat, Patrick opened the screen and accepted the registered letter. A bittersweet feeling overwhelmed him as he tore open the envelope. It was the final divorce decree, signed by Cynthia. He put the paper back in the casing and slowly made his way up the road. When Sarah Jane opened the door, she noticed his serious expression.

"What's wrong?"

"I got my final divorce papers today."

A smile lit up her entire face.

"Ya don't say! So did I!" She reached out to a coffee table and produced a letter of her own.

"Jus' after y'all got here, I decided to start lookin' for Damien's daddy to end this charade once and fer all. I found 'im and I had him served with papers! Don't God act in mysterious ways sometimes?" Patrick felt all of his doubts disappear. He grabbed Sarah Jane by the waist, brushed her dark hair from her blue eyes and beamed down at her lovingly.

"I love you, Sarah Jane," he whispered. Then he leaned in and gently placed a sweet kiss upon her lips.

"Pa...pa...pa...!" They both turned to look at Damien who had appeared in the doorway to the kitchen, pointing at Patrick.

"Oh! Damien is trying to say my name!" he almost yelled and quickly threw his hand over his mouth worried about startling the boy. Sarah Jane smiled dreamily at him.

"No, honey. I think he's trying to call you 'pa.' Will you be my boy's pa?"

And Patrick could not remember a time when his heart had been so full, his life so complete. *Thank you, lord, for giving me another chance at happiness.*

"Only if his mother will agree to be my wife."

# MOTHER ANGEL

## NIKKI CARLSON

"Mama! Mama!"

She was at the crib, leaning down over the inconsolable child, her hands gently stroking the damp tendrils of hair, curls that were soaked in sweat from night terrors.

"Shhh...mama's here. Don't cry, mama's here," Vivienne whispered, reluctant to pick up the baby even though every fiber of maternal instinct begged her to lean over and do so. "Go back to sleep now, sweetheart. It's time to sleep."

The little one continued to wail, small chubby arms reaching up, big, brown eyes swimming in tears.

"Shhh....shhh....shhh..."

The door to the nursery opened and Ryan hurried in, half asleep with red-rimmed eyes and an unshaven face. She could smell stale whiskey on him as he slipped into the room and she wrinkled her nose in disgust. He reached past Vivienne and scooped Lily into his arms. Vivienne was completely surprised by his presence.

"Mama!" Lily screamed. "Mama! Mama!"

"Ryan! Put her down! She'll never learn to self-soothe if you pick her up every time she cries!"

"Daddy's here, baby. Shhh...don't cry. Daddy's here," Ryan cooed, turning his back on his wife and putting the sobbing girl to his chest, bouncing her slightly.

"Mama! Mama! Mama!"

"Ryan! Put her back in the crib!" Vivienne demanded, angry he was ignoring her. What is he even doing in here in the middle of the night? This is a first!

"Mama!" Lily was inconsolable. "Mama!"

As Ryan walked out of the room he began to rock Lily, leaving Vivienne staring after him.

"Ryan!"

"I know, baby. I want your mama too," he whispered to her soothingly.

Vivienne blinked and stepped after her husband but as she looked down to ensure there were no toys obstructing her path, she didn't make out her legs. Slowly, her eyes traveled up her body from where her feet were supposed to be and she suddenly realized that there was nothing there. Whirling abruptly, she turned to look at the full-length wooden mirror next to the change table. There was no one there. She did not exist. I'm having a nightmare, she concluded.

"It's not a nightmare," the faun whispered in her ear. "You're dead."

Rain-like droplets of sunlight fell through the maple leaves. The smell of wood burning filtered through chimneys and Vivienne felt both nostalgic and borderline euphoric as the comfortable and familiar scents of autumn filled the air. It was her favorite time of year, the fall. She continued down the street, pushing the stroller before her. Soon enough it would be Lily's first birthday and all of the fun of toddler-hood would begin. The incessant babbling and the toothbrushes in the toilet, the temper tantrums and the endless test of wills. The new mother looked lovingly down at her dark haired, sleeping angel and smiled. But for now, Lily was a still a small, vulnerable infant who needed her protection and she intended to relish this stage for the blessing it was. As Vivienne turned the corner, her small smile of contentment faded. Ryan was home already. She steeled herself inwardly as she slowly made her way up the front walkway with Lily. The child was beginning to stir from her nap and Vivienne groaned inwardly. The baby's timing for waking could not have been more off.

"Hi?" she called upon entry. "Are you home?"

"Yeah, babe, in the kitchen," came Ryan's response from the rear of the house. Taking her time, Vivienne unwrapped her daughter from the carriage and cradled her gently as the child became aware of her surroundings. Inevitably, Lily began to wail. Vivienne felt herself cringe. Ryan poked his head around the corner and scowled.

"What's wrong?" he asked sourly. "Why is she crying?"

Vivienne swallowed her anger and forced herself to answer calmly. "She's six months old. That's what she does."

Ryan grimaced but did not bother to respond and returned to the kitchen, leaving his wife to console the waking baby. Vivienne followed him into the kitchen and began preparing a bottle, carefully cradling Lily in one arm. Ryan did not offer his assistance as he sat at the island, biting into a sandwich he had just prepared.

"You're home awful early," Vivienne commented, popping the nipple of the warm bottle into her daughter's mouth. Eagerly, Lily accepted it, instantly silencing her wails.

"Yeah, they're calling for rain this afternoon. All the contractors went home," Ryan answered. "What did you do today?"

"Lil and I just got back from a walk. We went swimming this morning. I cleaned up a bit while she took her nap."

Ryan raised an eyebrow and looked around the room skeptically but he made no comment. Vivienne felt her temper flare. *How dare you! You have no idea what it's like to be home with a baby all day long! You have no idea how much work I put in!* She thought furiously. But she said none of these things. Instead, she took Lily into the living room and placed her in her playpen as she suckled on her lunch. She turned on the television and found a nursery rhyme channel to entertain her daughter before turning to pick up the toys strewn about the floor.

"What time is dinner tonight? My mom is asking." Ryan appeared in the doorway, holding his cell and looking down at a text message. Vivienne blinked trying to recall what day of the week it was.

"Why is she asking?" she asked slowly. Ryan frowned angrily.

"My mom and Jamie are coming for dinner tonight. We planned this last week!"

Vivienne felt her blood pressure rise to an almost dangerous level. She had no recollection of making the arrangements. *That doesn't mean I didn't agree to it,* she conceded silently. *It only meant that* she had probably forgotten in the midst of the chaos that her life had become. The thought of not only cooking for her mother-in-law and her mother in law's new boyfriend but having to actually entertain them for an evening was insurmountable. Lily had still not learned how to sleep through the night so Vivienne was functioning on minimal sleep over and above the day to day trials and tribulations of child rearing. Of course, Ryan could not be bothered to ever get up with the baby during the night. That's not fair. Ryan works really hard. And Lily needs her mom right now. It will get better. It will just take time, Vivienne tried to reassure herself.

"Six o'clock," Vivienne told him.

Vivienne spun her non-existent body around to stare at the creature. She immediately noticed the horns atop his deer-like head, slightly taller than the two velvet ears poking out of his bald skull. As her gaze lowered, she noticed his forehead sloped eerily between wide, innocent eyes. It was the eyes which captivated Vivienne as they were no definitive color. They were gold, green, brown and purple but somehow uniform. Staring at them was making her lightheaded and somehow queasy. She continued to look past his lopsided smile and down his naked chest to his waist where two horse legs supported his lean body. Vivienne swallowed.

"Are you the devil?" she whispered fearfully. The half smile became an unsightly mess of cracked, yellow teeth as his chapped lips parted and he let out a howl of laughter.

"Oh! It never gets any less amusing! No matter how many times I get asked! The devil! Ah, you mortals are so unimaginative." Vivienne didn't know how to respond. She waited but in spite of the shock she had just received, she found herself staring at the doorway wistfully after her family. She suddenly recognized she was no longer standing in Lily's nursery but instead in a vast nothingness. She stood, invisibly with the faun, uncomprehendingly. The beast began to circle around her, half predatory, half soothingly, his long index finger extended, touching the area which would have been her face...if she actually existed. His deep, strange eyes fixated on her.

"No, sweet child," he cooed mockingly, "I am not the devil. I am your friend. Your one and only friend." Vivienne felt a chill at the words but she maintained her silence and waited. He continued to do the slow dance around her, sizing her up as if she were some lamb for the slaughter.

"You and I will become very familiar with one another," he continued. "We have plenty of time to get to know one another. Plenty of time."

Vivienne decidedly did not like his tone.

"I do not want to become familiar with you!" she snapped. "What am I doing here?"

The faun found her words humorous and began to laugh again. Abruptly he stopped, his unpleasant grin fading.

"You don't have a choice, child," he snarled. "You are bound to me..."

He paused a moment, his eyes sparkling with something sinister. "Unless you can find a way out."

Before Vivienne could question what he meant, he disappeared and she was enveloped in the emptiness.

The shrieks of laughter resounded through the neighborhood. Someone had released a bright purple balloon into the air and Vivienne watched as it floated into the almost cloudless sky. The winter had melted away into a glorious springtime and she couldn't have hand picked a better day for Lily's first birthday. Her nieces and nephews ran amok through the backyard among the other children, high off sugar and adrenaline. The bouncy castle was filled almost to capacity and Vivienne hurried over to shoo some children out lest the structure collapse from the weight. Ryan's mother stopped her as she passed her spot in the sun. Vivienne rolled her eyes behind her dark sunglasses.

She tried to prepare herself for whatever gem her mother in law was going to deliver.

"Dear, I hope you put some sunscreen on Lily. It's warming up quite quickly," she said to Vivienne in that condescending voice which made Vivienne want to strangle her. Vivienne arched an eyebrow. Is this woman serious? She asked herself.

"Gillian, it's sixty degrees," she replied. "It's hardly sunscreen weather."

Gillian shook her head as if to say "you don't know anything" and smiled sardonically.

"It's not the heat which will harm her skin, Vivienne. It's the UV rays. UV rays are – "

"I know what UV rays are, Gillian!" Vivienne said more sharply than she intended. "I will get some sunscreen."

"Oh? Are you sure you have some? I looked for some in Lily's room but I didn't see any. I can have Jonathan go to the store and pick some up." Vivienne followed her mother-in-law's gaze to her latest conquest, a man barely older than her own son. The younger woman couldn't resist the opportunity.

"Oh, no need to trouble Jamie. I have some in the bathroom. I try not to keep poison in the baby's bedroom." She watched as Gillian's eyes flashed with annoyance.

"You mean Jonathan," she replied flatly.

"Oh...what did I say?"

"Jamie."

"Oh, whoops...I guess I got confused...with all the...'J' names," Vivienne answered lamely. Inwardly she was giggling. Her mother in law's borderline promiscuity was a poorly kept family secret. Her momentary win was deflated a second later, however, when Ryan appeared with Lily in tow. She was bawling at the top of her lungs, face red and tears streaking her cheeks. Ryan roughly shoved the child into Vivienne's instinctively outstretched arms.

"What happened?" Vivienne asked, scooping up her daughter. Ryan shrugged.

"I have no idea! She babbled something at me and then started freaking out when I didn't react. I don't speak baby talk. You figure it out." Vivienne gritted her teeth and wiped Lily's tears from her face. I guess I'm going to have to, aren't I? she thought angrily.

"Shhh...what happened baby?" she asked the child. "What do you need?"

"Mama!" Lily wailed. "Mama!"

Gillian shook her head and snorted.

"You are spoiling that child," she said above Lily's cries. "You shouldn't coddle her when she's being a brat. In my day, we'd get a wooden spoon for behavior like this."

"In your day they didn't have Children's Services," Vivienne replied, bouncing Lily in her arms. She would not be calmed. In fact, her wailing got louder. Ryan was getting irritated by the noise.

"Lily! Enough!" Ryan yelled, glaring at the baby. Giving Ryan a scathing look, Vivienne spun on her heel and walked away from mother and son, worried she was about to say something she would regret the rest of her life. As they disappeared into the sanctuary of the house, away from the noise and relations, Vivienne had a daunting thought. If anything ever happens to me, this is who Lily will be stuck with to raise her.

"Mama! Mama! Mama!"

Vivienne watched helplessly as her daughter sat up in the crib, sobbing out her name. She had been crying for what seemed like hours but in reality, it probably had not been more than a few minutes. Still, Ryan had no responded to her.

"Ryan! For heaven's sake! Lily is crying!" she heard herself yell into the darkness. For a brief second, Lily's voice faltered and the baby turned her head upward to where Vivienne hovered.

"Mama?" she whispered.

"Hi, baby!" Vivienne felt invisible tears form in her eyes. "Can you see me? Can you hear me?"

Her dark eyes peered searchingly into the void, rosebud lips parting. Then she let out a feral moan so heart wrenching, Vivienne swore that she felt herself die all over again. The doorway flew open and Ryan ran in, tripping over the Persian rug. Picking himself up, he ran toward the crib.

"Lily! Lily are you all right?" He rushed to pick up the distraught child. "What happened? Are you hurt?"

He looked her over as he rocked, making shushing noises.

"Mama!" she screamed over and over. "Mama!"

Looking completely defeated, Ryan clung to the small body, murmuring softly. Another form appeared in the doorway.

"What is going on? Why is she screaming?" Gillian demanded.

"It's okay, mom. She had a bad dream. Go back to bed," Ryan answered without turning to face his mother.

"Well, it's difficult to sleep with a caterwauling child in the next room, Ryan," Gillian retorted, stepping into the nursery. "Give her to me."

Vivienne watched in anger as her husband handed over their child.

"Now, Lily, listen to grandma," Gillian began in her usual no-nonsense manner. "It is time to sleep." Of course, the toddler was far too distressed to heed any reasoning and her cries escalated. She looked at her father in desperation.

"Daddy! Mama! Mama! Mama!" she continued to screech. Ryan turned his head away so he wouldn't have to look at his daughter's anguish. Vivienne was appalled.

"Your daughter needs you! What are you doing?" she howled at her husband.

"Lily! That is enough crying. You will go to sleep now," Gillian stated firmly. She put the troubled child back into the crib.

"Mom! She's still crying. You can't – "

"It's for her own good. She has to get used to the fact that her mother is gone, Ryan. Now go to your room. She will cry herself to sleep." Gillian pushed her son gently through the threshold and closed the door behind her. Vivienne stood frozen in absolute disbelief for a moment. Did that just happen? Did they just leave my child, hysterical and bereaved alone in the dark? Beside her, the faun chuckled.

"This is why we will be friends for a long, long while," he reiterated, looking at his long, bony hands. Vivienne spun to address him.

"We are not friends now," she hissed, turning toward Lily's crib, determined not to be perturbed by the being. "Why would you assume we would be friends for any amount of time?"

Again the faun laughed.

"Ah, sweet child. You aren't listening to me. I am the only friend you have. I am the only friend you will ever have again at this rate." Vivienne felt a stab of fear despite her resolve not to be intimidated. She tried to touch Lily's saline soaked cheek but of course, the act was useless. There were no fingers to make contact.

"Why is that? Is this what usually happens to everyone after they pass on? Is this purgatory?" The faun looked irritated with the barrage of questions.

"How sheltered of a mortal were you that you ask such ludicrous questions? What is usual? What is purgatory? These are only words without sustenance."

Vivienne was about to ignore the faun but her fighting spirit in her would not let it go.

"I may be sheltered but at least I don't speak in a cryptic riddle. I have the decency to explain myself, especially when I can see someone might benefit from some clarity." Those multi-colored, enigmatic eyes sparked with both appreciation and annoyance. When he offered a smile this time, Vivienne instantly regretted her words.

"You will understand when you understand. There is nothing I can say to offer comfort to your plight. But I can tell you this; you should get used to my companionship because the way I see it, you're bound to be stuck here for eternity. And I'm the only one who can see you!"

I can't do this anymore. Vivienne stared listlessly out the bay window of the front room, watching the sun shower without actually seeing the drops tease the thirsty leaves on the front lawn. Lily was watching Sesame Street and flipping through a hard paged storybook of princesses on the hardwood floor. Every once in a while, a sweet giggle would escape her throat and Vivienne would abandon her reverie to smile automatically as their eyes met. This isn't fair to Lily. This isn't fair to me. I just can't live like this. The revelation had come the previous night as Ryan had come home from work. Lily had just begun winding down for bath time when he walked through the door, covered in drywall dust and paint.

"Daddy!" Lily yelled, jumping up from the sofa to embrace her father.

"Hiya, baby! How is my favorite girl?"

"Daddy!" she yelled again. Her vocabulary was growing every day but sentences had yet to come. Vivienne smiled at the exchange. She was, without a doubt, becoming daddy's little girl. Ryan ruffled Lily's hair affectionately and stood up to kick off his shoes.

"Daddy brought you a present," he told her, smiling. Vivienne's smile faded as Ryan reached into his pocket.

"Ryan…" she warned as he pulled a chocolate bar out of his pocket. "It's almost seven o'clock."

"Chakit!" Lily howled happily. "Chakit!"

Ryan shrugged and grinned.

"You can't say no now, mama," he laughed, unwrapping the candy and pulling off a gooey piece.

"Ryan, just a little tiny bit – "But it was already too late. Lily was scarfing down sugar like it was being outlawed. Vivienne frowned but did not say anything. Ryan saw so little of Lily with his late work hours. She knew that the chocolate was his way of bonding and apologizing simultaneously. Vivienne didn't necessarily approve but she certainly wasn't about to infringe on their father/daughter time. After fifteen minutes of wrestling around on the floor, Vivienne laughingly announced bath and bed time for Lily. A slight protest ensued but Vivienne hustled her small daughter upstairs and into bed. It took well over an hour to put Lily to sleep with the fresh amount of glucose in her blood stream. When Vivienne had finally made it back to the main floor, Ryan was asleep in the recliner, still in his work clothes. And Vivienne realized he had barely acknowledged her presence since he had arrived home. It hit her like a flood. They hadn't been intimate in months, not even a kiss good-bye in the mornings. He slept on the couch almost every night and at first she had justified it as exhaustion but the more she thought about it, the more she saw all the signs that her marriage had burnt out. Now it was only a matter of who would actually say the words.

"Mama! Daddy!" Lily announced, rising unsteadily to her feet and pointing at the front door. "Daddy!"

Vivienne realized her daughter was right; Ryan was home already. It was not even three o'clock and the day was clear. She felt a smidgen of alarm. She slipped off the loveseat to join her daughter at the front door. A moment later, Gillian strolled in, Ryan on her heels.

"Gamma!" Lily cried hugging her grandmother. "Daddy!"

Vivienne blinked, the feeling of foreboding growing in her stomach.

"Hello, angel!" Gillian called, leaning down to kiss the small cheek before her. "Hello Viv. How are you?"

"Gillian, what are you doing here?" In her surprise, Vivienne heard her rudeness after the words left her lips. Her mother in law's smile thinned.

"Nice to see you too, dear," she said, ignoring the slight. "I am here to watch my angel."

Vivienne looked behind her at Ryan for an explanation. From behind his back, Ryan pulled out a bouquet of light pink baby roses. Stunned, she accepted them, still not understanding.

"We're going out tonight, Viv," Ryan said simply, ushering his mother into the house.

"Why – I mean what's the occasion?" she responded, dumbfounded. For a sickening moment, she wondered if it was their anniversary and she had forgotten. Ryan smiled sadly and embraced her.

"The occasion is you are my wife and I appreciate how you hold this family together. And I know I don't tell you this enough but I love you very much." Vivienne felt her heart swell up with hope and she looked into his husband's sheepish eyes.

"I love you, Ryan," she replied. Lily clapped her hands gleefully and clamored to be picked up.

Gillian reached down to scoop up the child.

"Oh, by the way, I just started seeing someone so I hope you don't mind if Philip stops by this evening after Lily is in bed," she told them.

"Mama!"

Vivienne was finding it hard to bear watching this night after night. Ryan had stopped coming in during the wee hours, allowing Gillian to take over completely. Every night, Gillian would come in, lecture Lily gently and leave her to cry herself into an exhausted slumber. Some nights Vivienne would try to sing and talk to her young daughter but after that one time, her words had no effect on the toddler.

"Ugh, please cease that racket!" the faun snarled as Vivienne paced the room singing, waiting for Lily to fall asleep. "You sound worse than the child."

"You don't have to be here," she shot back. "In fact, I insist, please go!"

The faun growled. "I don't have the option. Someone needs to keep an eye on you."

"Says who?" Vivienne circled the crib, hoping her movement would catch Lily's attention and help alleviate her agony. "You already said I am stuck in this limbo forever. Why do you need to be here? Surely you must have other places you'd rather be."

"That, sweet child, is the understatement of the millennia. There are hundreds of places, no, thousands of places I would rather be but at this time, you and I are bound. There is only one way for me to leave." Curiosity got the best of Vivienne and against her better judgment, she voiced her question.

"How do I get rid of you then?"

He smiled that awful leer.

"I can only leave if you do leave first."

Vivienne turned to stare at him.

"What – "

Gillian finally threw the door open to the nursery stopping Vivienne in mid-sentence. She looked angry.

"Lily!" she snapped. "Lily, you must stop crying!"

"Gamma! Mama! Mama! Mama!"

"Lily, your mama is not coming back. You must learn to accept that." Vivienne was horrified at her mother in law's tone.

"Gillian, she's not even two years old!" Vivienne screamed. For a second, Gillian seemed to freeze. Her crown of dyed red hair lifted to the direction of where Vivienne stood with the faun.

"Do you hear me, Gillian?" Vivienne tried again. Gillian's pupils dilated and she slowly backed away from the crib. A shiver seemed to crawl down her spine and she shuddered.

"Sleep, Lily. Go to sleep," she mumbled, hurrying out the door and firmly closing the door so hard, it was almost a slam. Vivienne turned to the faun.

"She heard me," she said to the faun in surprise. He shrugged nonchalantly.

"It happens sometimes. It's rare with older mortals as they are conditioned by the poisons of your world and lose touch with their natural instincts. When your daughter's grief lessens, she too will be able to sense you but right now she is overpowered by emotion. She is also too young to understand her surroundings properly. It would have been better for her if you had died when she was four or five." Vivienne smirked.

"I'll keep that in mind for next time I die," she answered facetiously. The faun shrugged again. Lily was beginning to tire and Vivienne looked longingly at her as her swollen eyes began to close. She would give anything to be able to hold that small, warm body against hers just one more time, even for a short minute. She continued pacing the room again.

"I beg of you, cease all the movement! You're making me queasy," the faun growled.

"Do you immortals get queasy?" she quipped.

"I imagine it's a very similar feeling to nausea which you are giving me."

Vivienne sighed. "What would you have me do instead?"

"I find it odd that you haven't visited your husband," the faun commented blatantly. "Is that because you blame him?"

Vivienne stopped her laps of the room. He was right. She had not once gone to visit Ryan. She had not seen him but for the few times, he had come to check on Lily. *Do I blame him? Should I blame him?*

Vivienne could not remember the last time she and Ryan had sat down over a meal and conversed. They had a lovely dinner at La Piazza over candlelight and wine and talked about everything they had neglected discussing over the past two years. After dinner, Ryan took her dancing to a new Latin club. It had been years since they had gone salsa dancing and Vivienne felt ten years younger. They shared kisses on the dance floor like they were teenagers and danced with wild abandon. It was two o'clock in the morning when the stumbled out of the sweaty venue, drunk, giggling and very much in love once more. Then Ryan reached for his car keys and Vivienne immediately shook her head.

"No. We'll take a cab home. We can pick up the car tomorrow." He argued that he was fine to drive and headed to the car. Vivienne had paused, reluctant to make a scene when the night had gone so perfectly. They had rekindled their faltering romance in one amazing shot, just at a point when she was ready to call it quits. Was it worth throwing it all away over this? They may never get another shot to make things right. She watched as Ryan fumbled to get the key into the door of the Toyota and made her decision.

Driving home, she stared quietly out the window, the streetlights whizzing by and counting the blocks. Home was not far away when he ran the stop sign. She saw it happen in slow motion. The red hexagon zipped by and as she turned to call out in protest, the truck barrelled down on the taxi cab. A split second before impact, Vivienne saw their Toyota which was slightly ahead, turn onto their street. Ryan was home safe. And then there was blackness.

She crossed the threshold to their bedroom and was immediately overwhelmed by the stench of dirty laundry and old whiskey. There were piles of clothes on every item of furniture. The bed itself had been stripped of all its linens and in the center of the bed lay her husband, passed out drunk. Anger colored her sight. How dare he drink after what had happened? How dare he leave Lily to cry while he slept peacefully? In her fury, Vivienne desperately wished she could kick him. Instead, she crawled into the bed beside him.

"Ryan!" she yelled. The faun guffawed but her husband did not stir. Irritated, she lay beside him and stared at the ceiling.

"Viv! Viv I'm sorry! Viv! Please, Viv!" At once, the words flew out of Ryan's mouth in a torrent. Vivienne turned to him. He was talking in his sleep. "Viv, don't get in the cab! Please, Viv! Don't get in the cab!"

Vivienne felt sorrow wash through her as she watched her husband began to toss and turn. Sweat appeared on his brow.

"Viv, I'm sorry! Viv, please don't get in the cab!" Thrashing violently, his cries were getting louder. "Viv! Viv! Viv! Viv!"

As his voice reached a feverish pitch, the door flew open again and Gillian hurried in. She rushed to the side of the bed and shook her son violently.

"Ryan! Ryan wake up!" she yelled. He began to stir out of his nightmare, still calling out for his deceased wife. Slowly, bloodshot eyes opening, he became aware of his surroundings.

"Was I talking in my sleep?" he mumbled at Gillian. She nodded, stepping back.

"Sorry, mom," he said, sitting up. "It's the dream. It's always the same dream. Why didn't I go with her, mom? Why didn't I listen to her?"

Gillian did not answer and turned to leave the room. But as she did, Vivienne was shocked to see her mother in law's eyes full of brimming tears. She almost ran out and Vivienne realized it was so her son would not see her cry.

"Mama! Mama! Mama!" Vivienne lay on the floor under the window in Lily's room. The faun was sprawled out lewdly beside her, not by design but simply by the very nature of his being. She had given up on singing or talking to Lily. She saw the futility in those actions now She had succumbed to the helplessness of her circumstances and now allowed the depression to overcome her. She was waiting for Gillian's customary cold arrival and soon, Lily's grandmother appeared. This was only the first time that Lily had woken so far that night. This night, however, Gillian leaned over and picked up the child.

"Shhh.... grandma's here, angel. Grandma's here." Surprised by the turn of events, Vivienne sat up and watched as Gillian took her granddaughter to the rocker and lulled her back to sleep. Vivienne slowly walked over to her and watched as Lily nodded off.

"I know you're here, Vivienne," Gillian said simply. "I can feel you."

Vivienne was at a loss for words so she said nothing.

"We all miss you terribly. I'm sure you can see that. We're trying our best to get by without you. I know you think we're doing it all wrong," she continued in a quiet voice.

"You are!" Vivienne replied. She thought Gillian smiled but it was difficult to tell in the darkness.

"You can go, dear. Everyone will be okay. I will always be here for Ryan and Lily. And they have each other."

"Go where, you stupid old woman?" Vivienne yelled. "I don't need your useless advice. I need you to take care of my daughter properly!"

The faun cackled hysterically.

"You shut up!" she told him furiously. He laughed more loudly.

"Go now, Vivienne," Gillian said again. She rose out of the chair and gently laid Lily in the crib. "I promise, everything will be okay."

"Crazy old bat," Vivienne muttered as Gillian left the nursery. "She abandons my baby most nights, my husband is passed out drunk, completely ignoring Lily, the house is a pig sty. Oh yeah, if I had somewhere to go, I'd run right out of here!"

"Did it ever occur to you that maybe their world won't fall apart without you?" the faun asked casually. Vivienne whipped her eyes around to glare at him.

"Have you been here these past weeks? They can barely keep themselves alive, let alone Lily!"

"I suppose they are very fortunate that you are here then," the faun replied slyly. Suddenly Vivienne understood his point. There was nothing she could do to help them now. The only thing that would make them whole would be if she returned to them and of course, that could not happen. She blinked at looked at the faun with sadness as this realization settled.

"Will they be okay?" she asked, suddenly, hoping that he would give her the absolution she so desperately needed. He shrugged his characteristic shrug and grinned.

"It appears that the only one not alive is you so statistically speaking, they are already in better shape – well from a mortal standpoint." Vivienne chuckled in spite of herself and for the first time, she shared a smile with the creature. He really wasn't so bad. Lily began to stir in her bed. Vivienne felt tears well up in her eyes. This was never going to get easier to watch. She could not do this forever. Lily let out a cry and Vivienne turned to look out the window at the black night. In the distance, she saw something shimmering, like a mirage. It shone shimmery silver but Vivienne could not make out what it was exactly. Lily's cries began. Vivienne began her usual pacing routine, trying to tune out the distress. Time will heal her pain. She will grow up and be happy and healthy and never think about me. It's a blessing she's so young. She will recover from this faster. She will be okay. Ryan will be okay. She and Ryan will have an amazing relationship. Vivienne was at the window again. The mirage was closer now, just beyond the neighbor's backyard, a floating orb of light. Staring at it made Vivienne feel calm in spite of Lily's crying.

"Do you see that?" she asked the faun, pointing out the window. But the faun's face had changed. His horns had retracted into his skull and he was only a smooth, bald head with two soft ears on a deer-like face. His eyes had taken on more of a gold sheen than silver now but they were still filled with all the colors. His lips were no longer cracked but supple and shiny and he smiled, beautiful, ivory and genuine with no sign of the previously held leer. He wore a white gown over his once bare chest and Vivienne noticed the tunic was the same shimmery glow as the light outside the window. She suddenly felt very light, floaty even. The faun nodded and reached out a hand to her. His gnarly knuckles were now soft, callous free fingers and she accepted his touch even though she did not exist. His palm warmed her to the core of her being.

"Are you ready?" he asked her, softly. Lily sat up in her crib, tears flowing free. Vivienne looked at her daughter's sad, anguished face and then at the faun. She was conflicted, almost afraid. Would she ever see her baby girl again?

"I don't know..." Vivienne whispered.

"You must be sure," the faun told her. "You can't come back to this place once you let go." Vivienne stared at Lily, searching her face for any sign that her daughter needed her to stay at her side. Please, Lily, give mama a sign, she silently begged her daughter. I will stay here forever if you want me to do that but I need to know. Send me a sign. Anything.

"Daddy! Daddy! Daddy!" Lily called through her tears. And Vivienne knew then that she was ready to move on. Lily had her daddy. She nodded at the faun through her own stinging eyes and they watched as the orb of light slipped through the walls of the nursery and toward them. The faun gently squeezed Vivienne's hand and together, they stepped into the shimmering glow of eternity.